Informant i

Sheri L. Harris

This book entitled "Informant i" is a book of fiction. Incidents and the dialogue within are the product and imagination of the author. Any similarities between "Informant i" and actual events, and persons living or dead are purely coincidental.

Informant i is a book about: the Klu Klux Klan's secret relationship with a member of the African American society.

Information e-mail address: Gdi104@aol.com

Foreword
By Sheri L. Harris

Working For Diddly
Landhour
Aaron "Genesis"-script
Five Degrees from Seventy
Reptile-script
Little Green Men
Thank you, Mr. President-script
Cirilla
Day of the Moon
21111-script
An Unknown Child
Why You Cannot Serve Two Masters-
The Conflict Between Theology and Divinity
A literary work on thought and insight about the study
Of God according to the Bible and
Why we cannot worship two masters- dissertation
Let the Angels Fly

Chapter One

Lon Roner was a southerner who migrated his way north after being raised in the fields of North Carolina. It was different back then. No big city or crowds of people and traffic to get lost in. People like him didn't work in offices unless of course they could afford their own and they didn't come from families that would suffer from the after-effects of slavery in oppression. He was for the most part sheltered because he lived in a poor area surrounded by fields and shacks. No huge houses with winding staircases and servants who answered the door as you would see in the movies. Day after day he watched his mother work as a domestic and never complain about her job. She worked although she may have disliked the people she worked for. Lon Roner admired white people and didn't seem to have any hate or dislike towards them. Even during the civil rights movement, it was as if none of this had any effect on him as a black man. His aunts and other relatives were resentful as a result of the white man having his way because his cousins were lighter than him and had the straight hair to prove it. They never tried to fit in or assimilate because they already knew that they were not "white" as a result they would always be treated as though they were black because, in the long run, that's what they were considered to be. Lon wanted to fit in with whites any way he could. He looked at it as if it wasn't his fault that blacks were uneducated and had to take lowly jobs to fend for themselves. It was the times he was in and he could care less. His goal was to leave the South so that he could go North someday to mix and assimilate with white people. His mother warned him of the dangers of being too familiar with white people, It was something sinister about the way they viewed religion. Blacks were still commodities and as long as they were seen that way physical work would endure and freedom would be a word without any real meaning. Maundy Thursday was like a commandment that many people like Lon's mother followed, they didn't want to disobey their master because it would result in ugly consequences. Lon's mother warned him about religion as she would take him to church and spend most of the day there on Sunday. This was not important to Lon as he grew tired of the preacher yelling, jumping up and down, and waiving his hand just to make a point that there was a God. Lon had already had his mind made up. He would not seek out God as his people were so poor the only thing, they were rich in was the spirit and he hated this. He wanted to go where the man would control their destinies and seek out a decent life for themselves. Sure, God grew their crops and tobacco but that in itself didn't provide enough wealth for them to get out of that two-room shack that they lived in and cook fancy meals instead of eating scraps or the worst ends of the meat that whites didn't want. It was a beautiful day when Lon's teacher said goodbye to her class for the summer and Lon was just sixteen. The draft was in full recruitment, and he knew if he went over convincingly he could make it, and he did as he was accepted into the Navy without even as much as a glance at his paperwork. In those days the food was horrible, and the hours were long. The Navy wanted young blood because anyone who wanted to spend many a night on a cold windy ship was welcome to it. Lon got to see the world without him having to pay for it, it was a courtesy of the government. It was here that he learned that there appeared to be a value in depending on the government to care for him and stipend his stay without him having to be educated. He grew comfortable with this notion and used it to do great many a thing. He decided to move up in the ranks. He did not want anyone looking too far into the fact that he left high school to find a way to assimilate with whites because he could no longer stand the segregation. He met a woman named Elkin Khan and they married briefly. She was impressed by the uniform he wore, and he was impressed by her color and the fact that he could finally assimilate by being with her. She was fooled by him into thinking that he was upward mobile and wanted to do for himself, but it was not until she had given birth to their daughter that he used the word Thursday and that was something that Elkin did not want to hear. She would think nothing of using their daughter as a sacrifice for anyone, so they had an argument and she left him. He pleaded that Maundy Thursday would be the best approach for what they had done because just a few years before in the southern state's marriage would have been illegal. He wanted her to understand, and he wanted to cleanse what those considered a sin. But she gave him no option and threatened to tell his Navy superior how old he was if he did not let her out of the marriage. He knew with a dishonorable discharge and without ever obtaining a high school diploma that it would be impossible for him to make his way up north to get a decent job. So, they parted ways in Mexico and soon after he was honorably discharged from the Navy. His commanding officer asked him to reenlist, but he declined because he hated the cold winters on the ship and the overnights they would assign him to. He wanted more for himself, and he wished that he hadn't blown it with his first wife Elkin. Had he listened to his mother instead of thinking he was so sure that all whites wanted to use Black people in Maundy Thursday things might not have ended the way they did, but Elkin was different, and Lon was wrong about her. He decided he had to be more careful next time because he did not want to anger some white man or have the woman say that he tried to have his way with her. No, this could not happen. Eventually, he found his way up north and got a job in a business office of a clothing store. This was where Lon saw people like him working in offices and not in overalls and other beat-up clothing and picking produce grown on their field and selling it to the local stores. The Navy had provided him with a good enough reference that the store never bothered to check his high school records. Although he was sure that the schoolhouse still existed, he knew he could never go south again because his teacher would wonder why he never even bothered to finish. Lon Roner had thought about his daughter and even wanted to visit her, but his divorce was a bitter one. Last he heard she moved out west to raise their daughter. Lon often felt insecure about himself given the fact that many people were born and raised in the city. They tried to rid themselves of their southern accent and blend in. These people seemed so determined, smart, and wanted to go places in life. They were raising families and attending school at night. This was an important thing. Lon found comfort in the South as he thought back to when he was a child. Not much was expected out of you except to do what they asked you to do. There were no goals or ambitions one had to set for themselves to make someone proud of you. If your family grew tobacco and you followed along by trade, then that is what you did. You stuck with it and the family and that was good enough to be proud of and no extra work was needed. In the city, the fields were gone, and you had to acquire an entirely new skill set. Computers were the in-thing and although they were not in every home the job required you to have more of a mental thinking capacity than a physical one. Computers were so large that they took up offices. The south was different, and Lon began to miss the South terribly, but he could not return because he knew that if he did it would disappoint his mother. After all, she wanted him to leave the fields behind.

Chapter Two

"Hello, young fella!" said a large white man with aged skin and rotted teeth.

Lon smiled cheerfully as he grabbed a cup of tea and was ready to leave the break room area.

"You must be new here. I've seen you around, but I didn't get your name." said the man as he smiled and lit up a cigarette.

"It's Lon Roner, I have only been here a few weeks," said Lon as he tried to hide his southern accent.

"We run a tight place here and we need everything to go accordingly. But you seem like a good fit because you do not look like the troublemaking type."

"Uh, no sir," said Lon who was puzzled because he was up North and people were supposed to be seen as integrated.

"Good, good!" said the man who took a long puff of his cigarette and looked around and noticed that no one else had entered the breakroom.

"You from here?" asked Lon reluctantly.

"Not intentionally." said the man who laughed out loud. "I'm a southerner by choice but I kinda made my way up North. You know many people left the South and well not much to do if ain't no rebel rousing to get into."

"But I thought you said you didn't like trouble," said Lon.

The man smiled as he observed Lon and the breakroom remained empty. "It ain't trouble boy." said the man.

"I can respect that," said Lon. "Would you like me to leave?" he asked anxiously.

The man giggled. "I'm sure you still got that Navy bag full of clothes packed and you ready to jump said on back South just as soon as somebody run you outta here." said the man. "Uh, lots of your kind be comfortable in knowing we not gonna expect too much out of them.

If they keep doing things the same way they will be just as happy as a watermelon. Green on the outside and full of seeds ready to plant on the inside."

Lon smiled. "Hey, that is a great name for a clothing store. I suppose the regular melons not gon give you much help."

"We still going by the gospel, ain't nothing changed with that. The problem is now we got competition from all over the globe, and we got to keep up with the rest of the world. We got imports coming in that will make our exports or made in America look soft, so when things change, we got to keep up with it. Which is why we are here." said the man who seemed slightly embarrassed.

"I will do my best," said Lon who realized he was in the breakroom long enough and was sure that his supervisor was looking for him.

"We gon work really good together Lon." said the man. "You're different than the rest of the melons."

"I didn't get your name, but you seem to know mine," said Lon who realized the area around him was quiet.

"My name is Kib." said the man who continued to smile. "Now do not you be so worried about what other folks say about me around here. We got them gossipy types that just like to chatter away and spread them wild rumors that end up getting them into a heap of trouble."

Lon laughed. "I have never seen so many dedicated and hardworking people around here. They seem to always be learning something or doing something to improve their lives."

"That's what I mean boy!" snapped Kib. "You know we expect em' to be a certain way and when they kinda don't want to cooperate that's what we call troublemaking. They always gossip about how to improve themselves. But they ain't nothing to improve they just need to be the way they were meant to be."

"Evolution of the mind," said Lon.

Kib grinned again and looked at Lon and said, "You're special."

Lon liked hearing those words and longed to fit in with people like Kib. He wanted to be one of them, but he had to find somebody who liked him enough to let him in.

"That's the first time I have ever heard that," said Lon who was so happy he did not know what to do with himself.

"You relate to me or people like myself the way we want you to. And not the way you think we wanted you to be perceived by us. That's the problem with these people. You feel if you so educated then we gon say all aboard front and center. True, we want them smart but non-destructive smart. We want to know what you need to know to do the job we tell you to do and work until we tell you to stop. We don't need any fanciness and you trying to conquer the world in the interim. That's all, there seems to be around here people learning, gossiping, and trying to take over. Cannot let it rule, just don't work that way."

"And you call that causing trouble?" asked Lon.

"Yup, you trying to be me and if you trying to do that then who am I supposed to be?" asked Kib.

Lon thought and he realized that was why man played God.

"So, I know why you play God, now it all makes sense. You have to be superior. I understand you." said Lon. "Now, we've talked quite a bit and I have to get back to work cause like I said I don't want to upset anyone, especially someone who wants to play God."

"You, gon on, now!" said Kib calmly. "We got lots to talk about, see you around."

Lon walked back to his desk as others looked at him and giggled.

"Now you know he was one of them sheltered southerners. He stayed on the land his family raised on and then ventured into town now and then and as soon as he came of age off to the service and then to the big city. He never spent hours in a day with people like Kib or he would know that they played God even when we didn't get an education other than that shack of a schoolhouse until we found relatives to live with up North and that was when we had a real opportunity." said one woman.

"Like everything else, they got to keep tabs on everything, so I suppose that if we come here so do more of his kind. Somebody got to tell him that he should keep his distance from Kib. Man is bad news." said the man as he continued to work.

"I wonder what they got planned for us here?" asked the woman.

"We can squash advancement!" said the man sourly. "Once them crackers get in, they see to it that we stay just the way we are for these so-called modern times we work but the concept if you will ain't changed a bit." said the man.

"But we educate ourselves." said the woman.

"I think we are going in the wrong direction." said the man.

"How so." asked the woman.

"We got to teach the young the timepiece of life. This land here was built off our backbone I know that the kings of Africa sold us here in exchange so that they could keep the portion of the land to themselves and rule. Such as the Igbo people who enslaved other Igbo people as punishment for crimes and payment of debts, and prisoners of war. Now I got a friend of my wife who lives over in Africa and they are chummy, chummy with the royalty there. The South Africans ruled long before apartheid in 1948. I mean I truly think we are naive to this shit if we think those Africans just up and decided to adapt their way of living to what was going on here in America. They were doing this shit on the down-low and got in with the black kings of Africa and then took the good out of the country so they could take over and the black king sold us over to the white man in America. The Atlantic slave trade, I just wonder where they gon send us next." said the man angrily.

Chapter Three

Kib had just come home from work when his wife Benita greeted him at the door. "Hey honey!" she said happily.

Kib was not too pleased he was looking for some sugar and although Benita looked good on paper and out in public, he wanted some spice.

"Uh, I got some running around to do," said Kib

"Dinners, ready!" said Benita as she thought Kib worked too hard at times.

"Wrap it up, stick it in the fridge and I'll get to it when I get in!" he said as he put down his briefcase and went to the bathroom and then changed his shirt and left the house.

Benita looked bored as he left and thought about their open marriage and how she wished she had one that was more than just paper. Of course, there were options. She could divorce him and be a single woman looking for love in the many bars throughout the city or she could do like many women who were afraid to be alone and hang in there since being married gave them an identity or purpose. Benita gathered the bills together and got the checkbook and looked at the balance.

"Hmm, seems somewhat low for what she and Kib were earning and it was as if they were living off of one income," mumbled Benita to herself. Their children were still young, and it became a struggle to keep the family afloat financially. She did the next best thing and searched around the house for more receipts. She found several more in her purse and then thought of the obvious. "Let me check Kib's pockets." Benita went through Kib's trousers and found several bank receipts that added up to over seventy dollars. He made withdrawals for ten or even twenty dollars at a time. She found some store receipts and what she dreaded but always knew, a receipt from a motel. It was as if she was doing laundry and found lipstick on his collar or perfume that wasn't hers. The feeling stung but she was not surprised. They married as a formality like many people in her day did. Lots of marriages were not out of love or desire, but the family element was important, and to create future generations was of value and many people played the pretentious game and kept up appearances. The banks were closed, and she decided to call to get an automated balance by phone.

"Now, if I pay all of the bills. I will close out our account," she said in disgust. Benita began to write out a check that was due immediately and then she decided that she would mention to Kib that the rest of the bills needed to be paid so they had to tighten up on things. But Kib would mostly ignore her when she tried to talk to him. He would just take whatever cash he had in his pocket and put it on the table and grab a beer and go into the other room. For the most part, it was the amount she needed to keep a roof over their heads. Within a few moments, the phone rang. It was Stace a co-worker who had a way of creating benefits for herself.

"Hey darling, how goes it?" asked Stace in her cheerful mood.

"I want a separate account. It's as if all of my money goes to taking care of the both of us and all he does is withdraw money for motels, food, and beer," said Benita in disgust.

"Not to worry, you still have a few years before he walks out on you." laughed Stace. "At least that's the way it was for me. We raised a family as soon as my youngest was out of high school he was out the door with someone our son's age. Sure and as, you know I cried for weeks but then I began to think that I had my life back and I didn't have to pretend to be in a marriage that didn't exist as far as love was concerned. Ok, it was gone on paper but that was all that existed." said Stace who lit a cigarette and smiled as if she didn't have a care in the world.

"Speaking of paper, two incomes are more than one. He left you without a way to support yourself. Don't forget for many a year you were a homemaker and when the kids got to a point where they could look after themselves with some nearby help you went out to work. Now you didn't make nearly as much money as Kib but you were able to be employable." said Benita.

"Sometimes you have to make your way and I'm keeping it real by saying we have to be smarter and stay off the streets." said Stace.

"For some reason, I think you have something in mind and want me to get in on it with you, but you were waiting for the right time to let me in on it," said Benita.

"You ready?" asked Stace.

"Talk quick, the phone bill is due any day and I have just enough money," said Benita.

"You know those old people care homes that we get approvals for from the state, which agree to pay a certain amount," said Stace.

"Yeah," said Benita.

"Lately we have been getting a lot of rejections. You know more than normal. They have changed the state requirements and now many people need to have costlier private insurance plans." said Stace.

"It's like putting people out on the street," said Benita.

"Exactly, so we thought of a plan to keep those people in their old folk homes despite rejection letters that we receive," said Stace as she grinned.

"What fairy godmother is going to help with this?" asked Benita.

"Our insiders are sending approval letters to these old people's homes so that they continue to keep them," said Stace.

Benita thought to herself that this was the silliest thing she ever heard of. "But how are the homes going to get paid?"

"Once the state receives approval letters from us stating that we agree to pay a certain amount. Then they will then pay what they are obligated to," said Stace.

"Well, won't the old people's homes realize that they are being short-changed, when we don't pay them due to a rejection amount from the state?' asked Benita.

"They are way behind on their bookkeeping and is the state," said Stace.

"What do you get out of this?' asked Benita curiously.

"A little something from the old folk homes we deal with. The state pays, our company pays and it will be years before they sort it all out. So, you want in?" asked Stace.

"I need to do something. These bills are piling up," said Benita reluctantly.

Kib sat in a chair smoking a cigarette from a motel outside of town.

"You know I was watching you all day and I couldn't wait to see you," he said.

"Look man save the mushy talk." said the woman sarcastically.

"That's what I like about you, you always put me in my place," said Kib.

"Excuse me!" she shouted.

"Well, you don't exactly yes sir to death. You come at me with all kinds of hate," said Kib as he winked.

"I never understood your people. We get out of slavery, and you still want in. Don't you get tired of laying up with our unwashed asses and whatnot? We got off them ships stinking like rotten dentures, but you were willing to do just about anything to lay up. And even now I tell you I got a man or even more than one and you don't seem to be phased by it." said the woman named Latrel.

"Maybe I like competition. I like controlling you and maybe I like having some fun," said Kib.

"Tell me something, when you marry and have your white family that isn't enough is it?" asked Latrel. "Because the minute you make it clear and have them kids your fake ass marriage is just that you know only for appearances," said Latrel.

"Well, you can certainly get to the point," said Kib. "We got to keep the race pure and secure and well we have an occasional slip-up, and we make one but we know how to use it for what it's worth," said Kib who seemed to expect Latrel to understand all he was saying.

"I get tired of you groping me at work, threatening me with my job, stalking me around town, and having me hook up with you at the most inconvenient of times. I got my kids cooking dinner for themselves and a man who thinks I'm working late," said Latrel angrily.

"Hey now!" said Kib. "It ain't all that bad. Your man is doing his running around with some of them mulattos out there although he claims you to be his steady. You are teaching the chitterlings of yours discipline so I don't see the problem." said Kib calmly.

"Look, I just want you to go away!" said Latrel in disgust.

Kib got up out of the chair and grabbed Latrel. "Now, dear you know that ain't gon happen. So just get that thought out of your head," he said as he tried to calm her.

"Are you done?' asked Latrel.

"For now." giggled Kib.

"Now you go on and clean up and get dressed and get on outta here. I got things to do," said Kib sternly.

Latrel got out of bed quickly and cleaned up dressed and left the motel without speaking to Kib.

Kib watched Latrel as she left the parking lot of the motel and caught the bus instead of a taxi because she didn't want the driver to ask her too many questions. Then he heard a door open to the adjacent room. Kib lit another cigarette and then asked, "You been here long?"

"Not too long." answered the man. "You were just about finished with her and..."

"And what?" asked Kib defensively.

"Nothing, I was just making a few phone calls." said the man.

"Don't tell me, you had everybody come over to listen to us!" said Kib who was slightly embarrassed.

"Just about and you pretty darn funny, the names you called her. I tell you one of these days that woman gon hang you." joked the man.

Kib smiled, "Nope, she just gets angry, but she doesn't have it in her to do such a thing." he said.

"Come on." said the man. "We got to hurry this meeting on up, we got more and more of them folk integrating into the city, and we got to get a hold of the bright ones, can't let them take jobs that they shouldn't have."

Kib nodded in agreement. After all, he was a member of the Klu Klux Klan.

Chapter Four

Kib's daughter sat in class with several other students. She was a second grader and Kib's youngest daughter. She did not finish her homework and didn't care to. If there were an issue, she would tell her parents and they would talk to the principal and things would be worked out.

"Wendor," said her teacher Ms. Beckman, "Were you able to complete any of the assignments that I had given you?" she asked.

Wendor laughed.

"Did I say something funny or is that the answer to your homework assignment?" asked Ms. Beckman.

"My daddy tells me that I don't have to do it. We have been over this before," said Wendor angrily.

"But it's not fair to the other students." pleaded Ms. Beckman.

"They don't have to know. You are always blabbering to the other students and teachers that I don't have my homework done. It is not fair to me and It's and It's not fair to Kayleen. You always ask us questions in class. Why do you bother us so much?' asked Wendor.

"I want all of my students to be smart!" yelled Ms. Beckman.

"Then ask the smart ones and leave me and Marley alone." snapped Wendor. "You're no fun and you give us too much work."

"I gave all of you the same assignments. Why is that so difficult to understand that I treat all of my students the same, Wendor?" asked Ms. Beckman.

"Because we're not!" said Wendor.

"Why are you not the same?" asked Ms. Beckman curiously.

"We look different, or didn't you notice," said Wendor.

"Should that matter?" asked Ms. Beckman as she looked over at the other students.

"My daddy says it does," said Wendor without worry.

Ms. Beckman grew angry. She knew her job as a teacher would be challenging but when you have families who teach their children religion and values that are in many ways biased then the children or the next generation will be that of their parents and progress between the races and different types of people would never exist. It was bad enough that the gay and lesbian community in the early days used civil rights to piggyback off of when they needed help in their communities. She knew that once gay people in some respects threw others under the bus to save themselves it was teaching them a disregard for humanity and not doing enough to educate people on how to care for themselves and take responsibility for their actions. It was unfair to act barbarically in a sexual sort of way even if you were not married and then use someone to help you once the repercussions of sin were too much for you you bear. Blacks and African Americans suffered tremendously. They still had not earned separate but equal treatment and became victims of oppression all over again when the religious undertone had taken over as a call to order human sacrifice as a result. Communicable diseases were like the second coming in that people of color endured and sacrificed for who they are and then the dynamic of tolerance entered the ecosystem and affected everyone. Things were rough and many people went along to get along as such it became a way of life. She looked at Wendor who was looking at a picture book. For an eight-year-old Ms. Beckman knew that Wendor had learning issues that were swept under the rug for the sake of her color and to save face with the other students who were able to do their homework assignments without too much trouble. Ms. Beckman remembered a parent-teacher conference she had with Wendor's parents, and she suggested Wendor be tutored after school on her subjects Kib told her that it was her job to teach and why should he pay someone else to do her job. That was when Ms. Beckman got the idea that perhaps if Wendor wanted to not do homework then maybe she would be more comfortable around those who she thought were destined to drop out of school.

"Ok, I will no longer call on you in class," said Ms. Beckman.

"Will you stop calling on Kayleen, also?" asked Wendor.

"I will stop calling on her too."

"Good, now can I go and play now?" asked Wendor.

Ms. Beckman thought and realized the severity of what she had done. If she stopped calling on them in class and then she allowed Wendor and Kayleen to stop doing assignments people would ask questions. Especially where tests were concerned. She knew she could do a student's test and then hand it back to them as though they had done it themselves because once they had to complete their standardized testing it would not add up.

"Wendor you have to try and do something, it's not fair to the other students," said Ms. Beckman.

"Ok, I'll ask my daddy," said Wendor.

"And I will go to principal Marshman." said Ms. Beckman.

"Why him, he doesn't know much and is always around the pretty women in the building and is never in his office when his wife calls," said Wendor.

"How do you know that?" asked Ms. Beckman.

"The one time you sent me for a time-out in the office near where the assistants are, I got to talking with a few of them. One of them went to school with my mother so we are friendly with each other." said Wendor as she looked at the clock." The bell is about to ring and you have to give out your dreaded homework assignments.

Ms. Beckman thought to herself as she knew she had to warn principal Marshman not to be too friendly because Wendor and Kayleen may get the school in a lot of trouble if their parents didn't promote them along with the rest of their class. It's true that many households have more than one child and it is difficult to spend equal amounts of time with each one of them along with the other things you have to do. These parents needed help, and tutoring had to be the answer.

She quickly handed out the homework assignments and the bell rang. Ms. Beckman hurried to the principal's office where she found him chatting it up with the assistants who seemed to be in a hurry to leave.

"Principal Marshman, do you have a moment?" asked Ms. Beckman.

He looked around reluctantly. "Wait in my office, I will be there in a few." said principal Marshman.

Ms. Beckman did as the principal requested and waited in his office.

Principal Marshman scurried over to a young office worker. "Uh, look give me a call later we can talk about your process for remedial learning and transitioning applied autism into skill sets for technology. I find you fascinating!" he said happily. As the woman looked at him and winked as she turned off her typewriter before leaving for the day.

He walked into his office and left his door open slightly. "I don't have much time I have to get home and then I have a few errands to run. " said principal Marshman. "What can I do for you?"

"We need to put the students on different levels, they can't keep up and as a result, they do no work and expect me to pass them along," said Ms. Beckman anxiously.

"So!" shouted principal Marshman. "They are kids, and we have to let them be. We're not all the same you know," he said as if he didn't want to be bothered.

"Great, I will just fail them. You know Wendor and Kayleen!" she said happily. "What a relief. At first, I thought you were going to find a way to put them categorically into a level they will be able to thrive without the pressure of the work that would normally be expected of them. Now that you don't give a grade of shit. I can just fail them until they stutter constantly repeating the same grade." said Ms. Beckman angrily.

Principal Marshman took a deep breath as he always did when he was making a quick decision. "Did you say Wendor and Kayleen?" he asked.

"Yes," she said politely.

"I don't think that would be trend worthy. Because if you flunk them, these parents are going to have to bring their kids to work every day and Lord knows if they bring them to work they will probably put the company out of business. Uh, give me a few I will get back to you. Don't want to upset their parents. I have something else in mind. Thank you Ms. Beckman and have a good evening." he said.

Ms. Beckman left the office as she smiled politely.

Principal Marshman looked for Wendor's phone number and contacted her father Kib at his office. "Uh, hello I am so happy I got a hold of you and you're not in the breakroom. Uh, you are still chatty with Lon?"

"Yup!" answered Kib.

"Good, good. Keep doing that," said Principal Marshman.

"Is Wendor ok?" asked Kib.

"Oh, she is just fine. A pleasure to have and typical young American kid," said Principal Marshman.

"What's going on?' asked Kib.

"Uh, nothing. I just want you to observe Lon and get him to go along with me on this one. We were concerned about our future and I think I have an answer!" said Principal Marshman.

Chapter Five

"It's late," said Mrs. Jacel Roner who began to worry as she waited for Lon to arrive home. Although there were times he would call for the most part there were those times that he stayed out for hours and would come home very late. She hoped he was ok and tried not to worry. Quezel and her younger sister Teneil were playing and she knew it was time for them to go to bed.

"Quezel, Teneil are you getting ready for bed?" asked Jacel.

"No!" they both answered.

"Why, not. It is getting late, and you have school tomorrow," said Jacel.

"We're waiting for daddy," they said.

"Uh, he's coming home late, and you need to get to bed. Don't worry he will look in on you once he comes home," said Jacel as she tried to convince herself for her children's sake.

"I'm staying up!" yelled Quezel. "I'm not tired, I don't care about school, and I want to see daddy."

"Did you guys do your homework?" asked Jacel.

Teneil answered first as she had just finished playing with Quezel. "Yes, it's all done."

"Quezel, did you do yours?" asked Jacel.

"Teneil, just said that it was all done. Why do I have to answer you also?" asked Teneil

Jacel went into the girl's room and looked at Quezel pathetically. "Quezel let me see your homework," she said calmly.

"It's time for bed now make up your mind," said Quezel.

"I want to see your homework!" demanded Jacel.

Teneil watched the both of them nervously. She knew Quezel was lying because she knew she didn't do her homework and it was as if she never had any. Teneil would come home from school and feel all kinds of pressure for one so young. It was as if the teachers were giving her extra homework or showing her advanced schoolwork. She cried at times because she felt overwhelmed. Quezel usually got out of doing her chores and did very little around the house. She had an excuse for everything and would even fake illness so that she didn't have to do anything around the house or in school which meant of course that Teneil would have more to do when it came to homework and chores because penance was a big deal and it had to be done by somebody so that when they decided who would pay the piper so all debts were paid.

Quezel got up under the covers and closed her eyes. "I didn't have any," she said quietly.

"Then why did you tell me it was done?" asked Jacel curiously.

"To get you off my back," said Quezel angrily. "You're always hassling me and giving me a hard time, so I have to tell you something to shut you up!" snapped Quezel as she rolled over.

Jacel became angry as she looked at Teneil. "Do you find this funny?" she asked.

Teneil knew this was coming. Whenever Quezel did or said something that Jacel didn't want to respond to as she should Teneil was in line for penance as a result.

"No, but you could have asked her the same question," said Teneil calmly. "She said she didn't have any homework."

"So you asked her?" asked Jacel pathetically.

"Well, I started to do mine and I said we could do ours at the same time but she told me she didn't have any to do and that the teachers didn't give her any. So, I continued to do mine," said Teneil as if she was bothered and couldn't understand why her mother didn't get in contact with Quezel's teacher if she suspected that there was a problem or why didn't Quezel's teachers call their mother if something was wrong.

"All I ask is that you help her if she has any problems and cannot do it on her own. For goodness sake you are sisters and you should help each other out," yelled Jacel.

"Ok, I will do that!" said Teneil as she began to become very tired. "Can I go to sleep now?" she asked. As she looked over at Quezel who had already fallen asleep.

"I have something I need you to do as in chores. This room is a mess and I want it cleaned now!" said Jacel.

Teneil got up and began to clean and organize the room. Although she knew why her mother was doing this. Secretly she wanted her to stay up and wait for her father to come home but she didn't want to come out and tell her that. She knew that her mother was worried and wanted Teneil to do the chore thing to have him come home and to make sure he was ok. Teneil knew that men would do their thing regardless and the cleaning was a way for her mother to get out of her responsibility of doing things like making sure Quezel had her homework done and keeping the house clean and if she did this she would not be so preoccupied with him coming home so late. Teneil continued to clean as she was exhausted. She quietly closed the door to the room and turned off the light. She was nervous but within a few minutes she heard what sounded like someone coming in the front door and she heard her father's voice. Teneil was relieved. Her mother could stop worrying and so could she at least for now. She heard her father say he had to work late and got too busy for him to call and he asked were "the girls" asleep" as her mother acted as if had it all under control. "Yup, they did their homework and went to bed hours ago."

"Good!" said Lon.

It was late and Kib knew that Lon had just gotten home from work. "I'll call him in the morning," he said. As he waved goodbye to his mistress and left the motel. Kib drove home and thought about his wife as he got closer to home. It was a man's thing to see other women and the woman's job to take care of the man as long as he took care of her. But if he was doing what he was supposed to do Benita would not have to work. Kib's philandering meant that his money went elsewhere instead of home, and he began to worry about what Benita would do once she got tired of complaining. She wasn't educated enough or even skilled enough to leave him and take their children. Benita's parents and other relatives were in no position to help her and move in with her. Kib took solace in that fact and decided not to worry. Benita knew what she knew and she knew that Kib was not working late. He was out and about with one woman that he had been seeing for quite some time. It was embarrassing at first because Benita found out through a friend of a friend that Kib had taken up with the ole boy's group and began to see women in a taboo sense. She knew these women were not the ones you marry.

"I have to get from under these bills. I feel like I am the only one working," said Benita as she continued to talk to Stace.

"Look we have a few facilities that are going to get paid instantly if you just send them the approval letter," said Stace.

"Then, how do I get paid?" asked Benita reluctantly. "It's going to look funny if I receive paychecks from agencies that I don't work for. What am I supposed to tell my accountant, that I am a consultant for these places?" she said as she laughed."

Stace was trying to convince Benita that this was a good opportunity to get some quick money off the books and use it to save for herself instead of putting her paycheck in the bank with Kib's and having Kib spend it all on booze and women. It wasn't fair to her or their children. Stace's husband did the same thing and she learned how to go for herself so to speak and she was just helping Benita do the same thing.

"It's a cash-only business. There's a girl who gets the payoff once the approval letters are issued and the agencies submit these letters as proof of approval when they submit their claims in for payment," said Stace.

"Look I'm no auditor but won't these things get audited?" she asked.

"Like I told you before. Do you know how behind we are in audits?" asked Stace.

"No," she said as if she did not want to know.

"It will take years for them to figure out what was going on. Nobody in that department does their job efficiently. People are always disputing denials, and nobody ever likes to contact agencies about their payments. People call out and there is barely enough staff to do the work available. People leave or quit and are not always in the know about what they are doing. Benita this is money that I don't have to think about in terms of making." said Stace convincingly.

"Ok, I will do it," said Benita.

"Great, there are lots of letters and we have someone on the inside who handles accounts payable so they know what the company does not like to pay for and will reject, so if we can get a portion of these letters out that we approve, we can keep the agency going and keep ourselves afloat with what they pay us and have the company make less of a profit because when have you known them to share the wealth? asked Stace.

"Hardly ever," said Benita as she laughed.

"Then it all makes sense. We are under-appreciated workers whose skills and talents are overlooked. So, we use them where we see fit. Now I have some letters I can show you how they need to be done." said Stace who looked over at the clock and realized that it was getting late and she knew her new husband would be home soon.

"When can you show me?" asked Benita.

"When we get in tomorrow," said Stace.

"Then when do I do the letters that you want me to do?" asked Benita.

"When you can just do them as though it's regular work. It will look seamless as like it's from the company directly so that no one will be suspicious and we can all earn extra money aside from what the company pays," said Stace as she saw her husband come in through the front door. "Gotta go, guess whose home?"

"Ok." said Benita, "We'll talk later." Benita hung up the phone and saw Kib pull up in the driveway. She hurried upstairs and acted as though she were getting ready for bed hoping he would have a drink and fall asleep on the couch.

Chapter Six

"That's correct!" said Mr. Deivers we are a school for mental functional challenges. "How may I help you?"

"I was calling to let you know that our organization has some students that we want you to see if they would be a great fit for your institution." said the woman.

"Well, I will have my secretary set up an appointment for them and we will see what we can do," said Mr. Deivers. "But what is the payout, you know any minority compensation? that money spreading like sugar nowadays?" he said as he laughed.

"I just interviewed several minority women whose children's needs meet the requirements of your program here and according to their family earnings they qualify to receive state funds that will be paid directly to you, so it is in our best interest because you can get more from the system based on the fact that you are willing to accept minorities. It will provide you with extra incentives that the school can either write off during tax time or apply for educational stipends for therapy and help keep the school going." said the woman whose name was Ms. Carteen.

"Good, good!" said Mr. Deivers approvingly. "But something puzzles me about all of this and you offering me free money for these kids. I take it you want something from me, but you are afraid to ask. Now I've known you for quite a while, so out with it!" said Mr. Deivers who wanted all cards on the table so that he knew who and what he had to deal with.

Ms. Carteen shrugged and giggled. "You know our little code on white nationalism in that we leave no white behind so to speak," she said politely.

Mr. Deivers nodded, "Yeah, what about it?"

"Our schools are having a devil of a time getting students to pass and get promoted as usual," said Ms. Carteen reluctantly.

"Where did you hear this?" asked Mr. Deivers curiously.

"We work closely with the board of education and the teachers are having to just pass several of the students along without the regular testing that comes with the territory, or if they take a test they have to adjust the grades," said Ms. Carteen.

"Well as long as we can get them out of high school we can send them off to community college or a business or trade school-like atmosphere and just leave it at that," said Mr. Deivers as if that was the least of his problems. "I say that to mean that not everybody from your school district will be made to become a senator or the founder of some big-wig company that nobody has ever heard of. Can't we get the tutoring or after-school assistance for these kids so that they can do the work that is required and expected of them, instead of passing them through?" asked Mr. Deivers angrily.

"You know that code on white nationalism." said Ms. Carteen.

"We've been over this before, what about it?" asked Mr. Deivers.

"White nationalism just has the kids to continue the race and keep the race as pure as possible. White nationalism does not raise children as disciplinarians because we see them as doing no wrong. We may use the word punishment to make it look good but we don't do things as severe like taking a switch off of a tree and giving a kid a good whipping that he or she will never forget."

"Go on!" said Mr. Deivers.

"When it was brought to the attention of the parents of these students that their children were falling behind and not doing their homework and remedial classes or lessons would be needed, they rebelled like slaves on a plantation. These parents hollered and insisted that their children were smarter than what we were giving them credit for and in doing so they also accused the board of education of bias," said Ms. Carteen

"Bias?" asked Mr. Deivers. "Your school district so stank you got more minority dropouts than the county jail got inmates."

"And to be honest that's the way we like to keep it. We use them to focus on the negative and pass our people along, but it seems as though we seem to be having a lot of issues with students going to another school district, getting GED's or even dropping out and going to work with family members and we cannot set this type of standard," said Ms. Carteen.

"The bottom line is that once these kids get out of high school they are out of our hands and thank goodness," said Mr. Deivers. "We have enough trouble with people who lack a certain aptitude and functional abilities that we somehow have to occupy them and then transition them to different living modes away from their parents. This is not an easy task."

"I know and it's not easy when we are bombarded with students that fail to pass core competency tests. But these are our kids that will go out into the world and may not be able to compete with the technology new and future and it would be embarrassing for them to go out into the world and just flunk at it all together and then you have employers who ask what school did they go to?" said Ms. Carteen. "It's a reflection."

"So you mean if you pass the students along like popcorn in a movie theater then at some point when all they produce is kernels that nobody wants to eat them and employers will either find a way to put these people on disability because of their lack of aptitude," said Mr. Deivers as if he was beginning to understand.

"Exactly!" said Ms. Carteen, "I mean we have had some students return to the district, not as a student of course but our board of education also offers adult courses for certain skills outside of the traditional classroom. We do this because we don't want to be flagged for any audit."

"Did you say, audit?" asked Mr. Deivers.

"Uh, yes. If it is found that a student or rather a former student ends up on disability due to aptitude issues then the schools are flagged for not noticing that it existed while the person was a student. The problem becomes when these people are tested and it is found that they are unable to do the basics of things and it is then connected back to the school who of course issued them their diploma. That is how they know we are just passing them along in the white nationalist way. said Ms. Carteen.

"Does this audit by any chance go to the state?" asked Mr. Deivers curiously.

"It most certainly does. That is who conducts the audits because to pay out the disability they need to justify or have proof of the reason as to why a person is unable to work so they test a person at a high school level or even basic college knowledge and the person fails the test and they have a high school diploma that states they can do a certain level of work, the state then audits the school district and asks what happened. My organization like I said before because we work closely with the board of education has doctors that we pay to give a diagnosis of early onset of dementia because we can never fess up to the fact that we allowed these students to just pass through without doing the work that is required," said Ms. Carteen.

"Look this sounds kind of deep and if those that audit the board of education ain't sniffing turpentine surely they will become suspicious if all these people seem to have an early form of dementia just so that they can collect disability and save face about the work that they never did in high school or any other grade so that it does not look like there is an aptitude issue," said Mr. Deivers who began to worry knowing that when there is a doctor involved things cost more money.

"There was no way out of this because we needed a diagnosis to keep the audits at bay and from them doing..." said Ms. Carteen as she did not finish her sentence.

"Doing what?" asked Mr. Deivers. "We're white nationalists, so what if we pass our own and a red flag goes off, what can they do to you?" asked Mr. Deivers.

"We will have to provide the same courtesy to other minority students," said Ms. Carteen and that is something we don't want because we have our standards and rules no matter how double they may be.

"I'm beginning to see the picture. So where do I come in at? You seemed to have designs on what you want me to do."

"In addition to the people who have aptitude challenges we come into contact with siblings who are of higher function and we can use them because we see them as a great resource," said Ms. Carteen.

"You mean," said Mr. Deivers.

"Yes, we have to find a way to structure the workforce so that these people will work alongside those with aptitude challenges so that they can avoid going on disability and the board of education won't get audited and fined or even shut down due to poor grade performance," said Ms. Carteen.

"How do I do that?" asked Mr. Deivers as he pretended not to know.

"Kib, will be in contact with you," said Ms. Carteen.

"So you know?" asked Mr. Deivers slightly embarrassed.

"Yes, our roots are deep and some of us just ditched the hoods, but this has to be done. It's embarrassing and humiliating as hell to have smart and intelligent or even gifted minorities out there working while our people in superiority are not able to do the same thing. We have to get a grip on this thing and the sooner we do so, the sooner we can continue our rightful place in society." said Ms. Carteen.

Chapter Seven

Lon Roner listened intently as a group of Black people were talking. They hated Endico Hall. Endico Hall was a clothing store that was upscale, very overpriced, and catered to the wealthy or well-to-do. Endico Hall sold everything that someone who could afford it would buy. To keep costs low Endico Hall hired blacks and other minorities to help operate the company so that could keep costs down. Endico Hall solicited top designers and had their goods manufactured for next to nothing overseas. Blacks complained the company never offered its employees a company discount or had a freebies bin for items that were returned and were never sold afterward. Endico Hall was cheap because their employees were not paid for days off except for the usual vacation pay and since they were closed on holidays their employees should not look to be paid for them. This encouraged workers to eat and drink responsibly because when employees overindulged during the holidays they would be too sick or tired to come in the day after and would expect to be paid for a sick day. Endico Hall was rather skimpy with raises as well because they felt that many people were living beyond their means and they knew the more they paid their employees the more they spent.

"So I hear they got some top designers who finish a product line of clothes dedicated to the forties." said one woman. "This does not make much sense. The clothes were hardly casual and without raises or bonuses how can anyone afford to go out and wear them?" said the woman.

"They got wealthy shoppers from all over the globe who put their shit that they sell here simply because this is an American store." said another man who continued to clean the floor.

"Tell me something."

"What?" asked the man who was cleaning the floor.

"Your wife also works in cleaning and maintenance in one of the stores, right?" asked the woman.

"Yea, they got her working twelve-hour shifts, and she is so tired when she gets home, I feel really bad. We had to move in with my mother-in-law so she could help us with the kids." said the man as he held his mop and shook his head.

"Are any of those stores crowded?" asked the woman.

"They get some shoppers during lunchtime mostly. But they get a huge number of mail orders that they have to fulfill through the warehouse and if they don't have it in the warehouse then they search for the item in one of the retail stores, but I have to admit they got many a store but not enough people to shop in them."

said the man as he grinned.

"You said they have a warehouse..." asked the woman.

The man looked at her as if she just got off the banana boat. "Yea, Lessy every store or business that caters to the public has to have a storage facility, otherwise how would they be able to receive and deliver goods?" asked the man.

"They never mentioned the warehouse during the training. This makes me curious." said the woman.

"Now listen!" said the man in an angry tone of voice. "Don't go flapping your gulls off during break time about it. I mean what they are doing in there is company secret and supposedly they got a heroin thing going on in the fabric of things and they also got some kind of adult entertainment going on. I got a buddy that works there." said the man who knew that he had told the woman too much already.

"Is he a bitch double?" asked the woman.

"What kind of lingo is that, you seem to be ahead of your time?" asked the man.

"Well, what does he do at the warehouse? If you got adult entertainment and drugs happening to have him work, there he must be a double of sorts. I mean the man, ain't gon go out and tell his wife he got to hurry up and get the next shipment of heroin in and recruit girls who need money to get by on hard times. What if she talks and tell somebody, we gon all be outta work?" asked the woman.

"I see what you mean. You mean he had to put on a front to make his work here look legitimate." said the man who saw Lon looking like he was reading a book, so he paid him no attention.

"Duh, you know Endico Hall has an outstanding reputation for high-end quality clothing for the rich and snobby rich and they can't have people know we got a warehouse room dedicated to distributing heroin to Chucky the street hustler who also is a numbers runner on the side. So what does your friend do?" asked the woman.

"He doubles as a bartender for the warehouse parties that the bigwigs throw monthly." said the man.

"So they discuss business?" asked the woman.

"For sure, a lot of the well-to-do also do them side gigs like hustling in heroin and they make a lot of money on that and other drugs. Endico Hall is no different. They prepare package deals so that when they send that fancy outfit to some actress's home, and they want some heroin they can have it all delivered together. They can stop wearing dark sunglasses when they go out somewhere to see if they can find a dealer to sell them some. Sometimes even famous people show up to these parties and they get certain perks for placing advanced orders on clothing and other items." said the man who realized he should have been cleaning the other offices by now.

"What kind of women are at these monthly adult gatherings?" asked the woman.

"The taboo kind you know exotic or not what they say to be in terms of color or nationality. So, you need not apply. I mean they got a thing for dark chocolate, but they won't go out in public with them. It seems to me that many of these people find it difficult to find jobs because people tend to pawn them on others for one thing or another. Pretty women and a few men, from what I understand. But that's what keeps the business rolling in with the money and keeps us employed. Without that wealthy clientele where would we be?" asked the man.

"I do not see where you are going with that question. You got Manny's Bargains which does a landline worth of business because of people like us who make very little money and have to raise families off of it. Many of us are single-parent households."

"Don't take the fact that your man walked out on you because he couldn't do a job to support you out on everybody else. I think you here because you found out that your man was out here dealing and he also deals on that street level with people known to be associated with Endico Hall." said the man loudly.

As Lon pretended to ignore both of them.

"At least things are evened out. You got a few rich people in wealthy stores spending a lot of money and you have many, many, many poor people spending a lot less money and that is what keeps Manny's Bargains in business. Now you know where my husband is so you best tell me or your wife will find out about that exotic affair you've been having..."

The man dropped his mop and stared at the woman whose name was Lessy. "You may be crazy at times, but I know you ain't stupid." said the man whose name was Davis.

"Look, I'm not going to give you a multiple-choice answer to this. But I know you know my husband and I want to know where he is and who he is with or else your wife finds out about your get-togethers at the warehouse because that's how you know so much about it," said Lessy.

"Ain't no sense in you blackmailing me like this because I was going to come clean to her anyway," said Davis. "You know me, I don't like to keep secrets from my wife.

"And that honor roll student daughter of yours that you say she's going to have to work her way through college unless she gets a scholarship because that second job you told your wife you are working is just you hanging out a bring home just enough money to support the family. You made your wife work extra hours as penance for your exploits as a man. You thought you had it all together. But you're a typical purple-hearted man who can only do very little just like my husband. I heard you mention his name and I decided to observe and follow you until you were able to provide what I needed." said Lessy.

"And what if I don't?" asked Davis.

"I will see to it that, your honor roll student daughter of yours will hate you for the rest of your life," said Lessy. "You said you are going to come clean to your wife but that is some bullshit in the making right there. I know it will break your heart to have that little girl hate you and she should."

"What's all the drama, I ain't done nothing to her?" asked Davis.

"Because you have been lying to her and the girl thinks your days are working so hard to put food on the table and all you doing is hanging out feeding your bratwurst in some alien poom-poom. You keep your wife working so that when she gets home she's too tired to know what's going on and what you're really up to. You are one said clown and I am going to put your performance to an end unless you tell me where my husband is?' said Lessy.

"I can't Lessy?" said Davis sadly.

"Why can't you tell me where he is, you've told me everything else," demanded Lessy.

"It's not something you can handle at the moment. Big Troy got a whole new life and he kept it kinda on the hush, hush.." said Davis.

"Why?" asked Lessy.

"Now come on here, do not be so naive with me. You know Big Troy left you for another woman," said Davis.

"I know he was seeing one during our marriage, but to up and leave is inexcusable," said Lessy.

"If you would just move on with it, I think you will find someone else and not focus on Big Troy. Believe me, you do not want to upset him by confronting him and his new family." said Davis who realized he told Lessy more than he should have.

"His new family?" asked Lessy.

"Yup!" said Davis reluctantly, "He got kind of a makeover in the way that he changed his name so that the state won't know he was married before."

"So, you think this is too much for me? said Lessy.

"What do you think, here you got a husband who doesn't want nothing to do with you and your children?"

Lon realized he had spent too much time sitting in the breakroom area and had quietly picked up his book and left for his desk as Lessy and Davis continued their heated discussion. He had to report this information back to Kib. His job was to let him know of people who could be of potential threat to the White nationality. Davis had a daughter on the honor roll and that has to be monitored. Only so many in and so many out. He looked over and saw a memo message from his wife. Lon picked up the phone and decided to call her.

"Hey, it's me, did you call?" asked Lon.

"Yes, I did, the school called again." said his wife Jacel.

"What about?" asked Lon.

"It's a public school, so they can't be asking for tuition," Jacel said jokingly. "They just said to call them."

Lon knew the phone call was about his eldest, Quezel who never seemed to have any homework. "Tell Teneil when she gets in she really should get started on reading the Times and the books I brought home."

"But she has other schoolwork," said Jacel.

"She has to be stronger, and she has to do this now," said Lon

"I will tell her," said Jacel reluctantly.

"Ok," said Lon. "I gotta go!" he said as he hung up the phone.

Lon began to do some work and would wait for the right time to tell Kib and perhaps use Teneil as a way to earn an invitation to those warehouse parties because he was an informant for the Klu Klux Klan.

Chapter Eight

Kib and Benita Drendel got into their car and headed to the Ivory Loyal Knights Association meeting. It was a monthly meeting that was held on the outskirts of town in a small house that was adjacent to a much larger house on the same property that was owned by the Logman family who sold wood and other wood products for fireplaces and outdoor self-made barbecue products. Wood was a hot and much-necessary item back in the day and the Logman family had it all covered when it came to purchasing already processed wood for fireplaces and do-it-yourself grills. As homes turned to furnace heating and grills used propane and charcoal the Logman family sold their interest to Pine Homes which specialized in wood products used in building homes. Their treated wood process was beneficial to Pine Homes because it prevented damage from structural fires as a result. Mr. Logman was always a meticulous billpayer and hated debt so he would often have a tab at the Randon Township City Hall and kept a balance so that he would never be late in paying taxes. He also had a will that did not include the large home or the property on it so when Mr. Logman died the family took what they had inherited and assumed that the property would be donated to an institution of sorts. It would take a lot to afford and maintain the property and none of the surviving family members were interested in the task of maintaining it. As time went on since the taxes were paid Randon Township City Hall sent over township workers to clean up the property so that it would not look like an eyesore to those visiting the township and if the property were seen as neglected it would become home to vagrants and squatters. Eventually, there was no money left to pay the taxes on the property, and the town was forced to decide on the property. It had also raised taxes of the town's occupants to pay for the property and then the town mayor had decided to use one of the houses on the property as a secret meeting place for their Ivory Loyal Knights meetings. The mayor also prevented the property from being sold so that the meetings could continue to be held there and they could conduct organizational affairs without the issue of a meeting place.

"When should we tell the children?" asked Benita who often felt guilty about leaving Wendor and Marlie home by themselves. But they had no other choice because people in Randon Township attended the meeting and if they did not they were mistreated by their neighbors and even family members who were also members of the Ivory Loyal Knights. They could also be disowned if they did not participate in the rituals of the organization.

"About what?" asked Kib.

"Life in general," she said as she watched the road ahead.

"Well, then they are your girl's deary. You got to set em' straight on the birds and the bees and not dating none of them." he said sternly. "Now you get a hold of yourself and keep it together. Don't worry they gon be some fine girls when we get through raising them." said Kib proudly.

Benita thought differently because he wasn't the one constantly checking on them once they arrived home from school and staying up at night with them while Kib is out socializing. She hated the fact that the men often preached one thing but chased after everything taboo and all the women were there for was to have dinner ready if and when they wanted to eat it and to keep the race pure. "I mean about the Klan, Kib," said Benita abruptly

"That ain't the birds and the bees, woman!" snapped Kib.

"Somebody has got to tell them," she said shyly.

"Look, the girls don't know it but we got the classes all arranged so that they ain't got none of them too darks in their class," said Kib. "Now, I lay downs the laws here in this family so you let me take care of this," said Kib.

"Ok, but I feel so strange as if they are going to find out from their other friends or classmates and in doing so it would make us seem like bad parents," said Benita who didn't like keeping secrets from her children and felt a sense of responsibility towards them and often feeling guilty for sometimes using people the way they were being used. The Ivory Loyal Knights felt that that was the purpose of these people and it was their mission to oppress them as if slavery existed. They had taken over the schools, neighborhoods, and of course the employment sector and lived their lives accordingly.

Kib continued to drive and then went along a dirt road leading to the back entrance of the old Logman property. "We're here now, come on cheer up we can't walk in there like we feel as though we doing something wrong. If we gon act like that people gon notice and then we gon be having problems with Wendor and Marlie and we don't want that," said Kib. "Now let's get on out of this car so that they don't think we want to drive off and ditch these meetings."

Kib and Benita entered the house as they were greeted by another member of the Ivory Loyal Knights, and he saw some unfamiliar faces.

"Don't believe I recognize them," said Kib to an elder member named Stamford.

"Yeah, they are not so new in town. Their names are Lanny and Mike Piff. They lived here for several years, and Mike is a long-haul trucker. They moved away midwest to be closer to Mike's family when his dad was sick but now that everybody's gone and Lanny's mom who lives here in town, her health ain't doing so hot they come back here for a moment. But he's thinking it's going to be a permanent stay because the company he works for got an office not too far from here so he can do long-haul trucking and not have to be away from home so much. Many companies still rely on trucking because airfare and travel cannot carry as much cargo on a plane and it is quite expensive." said Stamford.

"So what's on discussion for tonight?" asked Kib as the member grabbed coffee and food and went to find a seat.

"It's not good," said Stamford. "We got a call from middle-states."

"Middle states, who are they and why can't they keep their people in line?" asked Kib angrily.

Stamford begins to laugh. "No, Middle States is a commission that promotes educational excellence, and they conduct accreditation for post-secondary education institutions."

"I think that got to do with college and our kids ain't there yet. So why is that a discussion?" asked Kib.

"Because our children are flunking out and colleges are beginning to ask questions about how they got in and what kinds of grades our children got in high school and how did they get as far as graduation, if they cannot do work that ain't much higher than high school," said Stamford.

Kib thought and then said. "How about a tutor or someone who can help them through?"

The room grew quiet and a man with a hood on entered the room. He picked up the microphone and then said, "I ask that you all take a seat what I have to say is quite important."

Kib found where Benita was sitting and sat next to her. "I wonder why he is wearing the hood; we are all supposed to know each other here," said Kib.

The man began to speak. "Our futures are supposed to be sacred and unaffected by any race or creed of person that exists in this country. It is understood that we hold superior value to those persons and will not allow any newly formed status of a person in this country to affect our rightful position of authority and entitlement in this county. With all that being said our school systems are under attack by the very institutions that we praise for accreditation of them. The performance of the student's grades and progress has dwindled, and the schools don't look good if we don't put in the effort to make it so." said the man.

"Accreditation is voluntary, so why just not stop the process? We don't need anyone telling us that our children are not worthy and that we need to shape up or ship out!" shouted one woman. "That's what we tell them!"

People in the room clapped and cheered.

"Accreditation is a global existence and is being used and implemented all over the country. If we begin to pull out then we will let the other countries know that we are vulnerable and our students have a lackluster performance with their grades and their ability to do the work on a certain level. We cannot allow other countries to see the USA as a weakness when it comes to learning." said the man who poured himself some water and began to drink out of a cup."

"Then why, now?" asked another man. "It was us who excelled and wanted to show the world our brilliance. What has changed that we are no longer able to do so?" he asked.

"We have several psychologists working on this issue and other specialists studying the mind and what is causing an affliction of sorts to make us question and ultimately have to restructure the way we educate our children and have them function in the workplace and society." said the man with the hood. "As of now, I have no definite answers." he said solemnly. "But I can assure you that this will not cause us to be second-rate citizens by any means and we will begin the process to maintain our heritage." said the man.

"How are we going to do that?" asked another woman.

"We brought them here in ships and beat them and caused them to learn and educate themselves in building this country by skill and then through education we did the same thing in creating bright minds as these people were brought out of the fields and into places of business. We need a system to work within a system of people that we otherwise want nothing to do with." said the man.

"Let's just say our children aren't able to do college and they go out into the world and need skill assistance are we frowned upon as a society for having so many people on disability?" asked another woman.

"The issue here is that why should we allow this to affect the livelihoods of our children when we can use others in assisting them with skill assistance." said the man who remained hooded.

"I think we are paying for the sins of our past and for the people, we have killed and hurt and the damage we have done to our environment. This has created a legacy of life imitating art upon our beloved children and is the science of God as in doing unto others as they would do unto you. He has called us in sacrifice. Do we challenge this?" asked the man.

"If we succumb, we surrender, we are a people of man and will not allow the created equal theory to diminish our work. I declare this a meeting of action. But we have to be careful, if they go back to segregation, where will that leave our children? asked the man who finally pulled off his face mask and revealed himself. It was principal Marshman.

Chapter Nine

Trinity was a huge conglomerate of a health insurance company that prided itself on assisting the Medicare patient with long-term care needs in addition to being a managed care health insurance. Trinity Health Insurance collected premiums from its members and then invested those premiums in high-yield stocks. They kept the money in their investments for so long that they were late in paying their bills including their employees. Trinity Health Insurance also denied services for about every single request and had providers scrambling to assist patients with their needs in appealing everything from a doctor's visit to a much-needed glucose monitor. The secret was that Trinity Health Insurance secretly owned many of the products that they had their members use. They had their off-brand durable medical equipment line that included pharmacy products. Trinity would often purchase companies to save them from bankruptcy and then offer to reinsure them to keep them afloat. In exchange, they would take the company they purchased and rebrand it and take the money out of the company, and manufacture goods that members would need to rely upon them when they used their health insurance. Trinity was a silent partner in glucose monitor manufacturing and test strips, they also were in the long-term care business and operated several facilities. They made their money by having members purchase their products and going to their facilities instead of approving them for fancier digs and high-tech equipment. Trinity Health Insurance was cheap and they were a no-frills brand of health insurance that believed that good health was natural and that if you did the basics to maintain it and there would be no problem. Stace had decided to grab a quick lunch as she stepped outside to the food trucks that were lined up and she saw Bon Schumer who knew all about the company because he made a living by selling insider secrets, everything from stocks to real estate. Bon Schumer signaled over to her and she grabbed her sandwich and paid for it and walked over to him as she tried to pretend to know him as though he were a good friend.

"Hey Bon," said Stace. "How's it going and how are the kids?" she asked so that her conversation would not attract those who may be listening for business information.

"Girl, if I had a nickel for every time somebody asked me about my kids and how many times I duck and dodge child support I would be a wealthy man," said Bon who looked convincing in business attire as he whispered to Stace.

"What do you do with all of your money because I hardly see you eat anything?" asked Stace who didn't want to spend too much time with Bon because she would have to explain what took her so long in getting back to the office.

"I like to look good and maintain a perception of success. In that manner, my clothes, car, and living expenses have to be on point. Now, enough about how I maintain. I got some word that you need to know." said Bon as Stace began to eat.

"Which is?" as she tried to hurry because she had to get back to the office.

"The company has decided to manufacture their diabetes supplies and require the members to buy their own by paying out-of-pocket." said Bon. "Now, it would not be such a bad thing if those monitors were of the latest technology but you may as well stick yourself with a bunch of pins in a pin cushion to get the same results," said Bon.

"Aren't these meters all the same?" asked Stace.

"These meters are still using the manual dial of reading and it is like turning on the radio in other words. Members aren't going to be so happy," said Bon.

"Why not some of the fancier digital ones that are coming out?' asked Stace.

"They say the LCD screens are too expensive and they don't last as long," said Bon.

"So they feel that making these monitors with the old and unimproved technology will be of help to the members?" asked Stace.

"You know Trinity, they come down hard on people with conditions and ailments. Trinity is a reform school type of insurance company that teaches you a lesson about your health and what you should be doing to maintain it as opposed to doing what you want to do and letting the health insurance figure it all out," said Bon. "So, what they did was that when they took over they catered to people who were low income and those who were underinsured and could not afford any health insurance. If you have nothing when someone gives you something you may feel as though this is helping you because you are so used to doing without. So you take it under the guise that this is all going to be of good.

"So now we're dealing with the father or the insurance," said Stace.

"Correct!" said Bon. "Now they got all of these cheap products ready for members to use unless you want to request authorization and delay your healthcare by waiting for approval for something that most likely will not be approved or be given an alternative easy read monitor which is still manual because they do not want to approve the latest and greatest in technology."

"So now we're dealing with the son because there is salvation in that you are now able to access care for the types of ailments that you have. As opposed to ending up hospitalized or dead because you didn't know that your blood sugar was too high or too low," said Stace.

"Correct!" said Bon. "Now I have the father and son moving about helping member to member in showing them that they should be taking care of themselves and not letting themselves go just because they have health insurance and doctors and other gadgets to assist them. Trinity does not want people to waste thousands of dollars on a false sense of security or hope or even rely on things such as medications for a permanent solution. This is the handicap that people get into and it becomes costly to everyone involved which is why

Trinity ended up reinsuring many health insurance companies because they approved the latest and greatest products and healthcare facilities and they allowed people to see any doctor they wanted and no restriction was placed on the amount the provider was charged and some providers know how to bilk the system and eventually put the health insurance company at risk. Eventually, people began to realize that it did them good to take care of themselves so that they could get off of the medications and stop making their life and schedule of seeing doctors as though they are making a career out of it."

"So now we are dealing with the Holy Spirit, in that the spirit comes in and causes the person to see the error in their ways and as they begin to get off of the medications, eat healthier, exercise, and not abuse their bodies and minds, as a result, become healthier people," said Stace.

"Correct!" said Bon who watched Stace finish her sandwich. Members will follow a spiritual path to wellness and as a result, the healthcare system will be a healthier one overall because it won't be drained by those who are in poor health. Trinity strives to reform the healthcare industry by discretely implementing these initiatives into its mode of work. If Trinity spent through the nose on fancy diabetic meters and supplies they feel as though they would be hurting the member because they become reliant on technology and use it as if they are playing with a new electronic toy of sorts. The idea is to change your diet, and change what you do with your body so that you can have your body become an asset to longer living instead of an instead liability.

Stace thought to herself as she was happy that she saw Bon when she did because he gave her insight as to how they were working and she could use that information because she knew that there were more approvals that she would have to create letters for if other companies and facilities were to stay in business. Trinity had quietly begun to take over the health insurance market and except for a few others as the middle class dwindled people would be in the position to obtain low-cost healthcare because once they became unemployed, retired, or were on disability health insurance was expensive to pay for. Now she understood why they would give people such a difficult time in approving care in that if they felt that a person could improve without relying so much on health insurance.

"Now this is their war on socialized medicine. They want people to be civil in their approach to taking care of themselves and not use religion as the divide and conquer to all things. It's a cruel thing to put your faith or tenant into a person who is of mortal being and expect them to be of your salvation as you neglect and continue to neglect what you are doing to yourself. Socialized medicine is evolving as Trinity aims to educate people by the approaches to healthcare." said Bon.

"By having people rethink their health. So, what now?" Stace whispered.

"The thing here is that only with terminal or end-of-life cases will they approve anything because the member has no way of improving the outcome of their healthcare so once it is established that a said condition is no longer reversible then a service will be approved. So you have to get with your people and find ways to create the letters so that they can support instances of ailments being nonreversible, life-threatening, or end-of-life," said Bon.

"It was great talking to you!" said Stace loudly. "Tell your wife I said hello," she said as she walked away from Bon abruptly. Bon smiled and waved and looked around before walking into a store to look around.

Stace got back to the office and clocked in just in time. She saw others returning from lunch and she then saw Benita who looked at her as if she wanted to speak with her. Stace didn't want to risk having too many conversations because she didn't want people to think that she was arranging a hostile takeover. But she wondered why Trinity didn't consider themselves the hospice of health insurance companies. She knew that it sounded cruel but this is what it had come to in training people for socialized or civilized medicine. Stace continued to work and waited a few minutes before leaving. Benita seemed anxious as she finally was able to walk over to Stace as she was leaving.

"Look I have to get home to the kids, so let's make this quick. I did several letters and was told to see you about more of them because now we have medical equipment denials. I hope we're not getting in too deep." said Benita.

"Look let's just focus on the extra money because we all have bills and they have to be paid somehow. We can't rent living spaces for as much as it costs to have a cubicle in the office and the company can pay us to work from home somewhere in the remote future," said Stace.

"Not a bad idea, for those who are single, but where do I put my children?" asked Benita.

"Just drop them off at the motel with your husband. Mine won't be coming home anytime soon and yours won't be either," said Stace.

Chapter Ten

Lon walked into the warehouse and saw Davis behind the bar he smiled at him and motioned him over to the bar.

"Wanna drink?" asked Davis as he looked at him suspiciously.

"I will take a glass of orange soda if you have it," said Lon as he watched the various men and women who were entertaining them.

"All you want is a soda?" asked Davis.

"Is there a problem with that?" asked Lon slightly aggravated.

"No, but you may want a stronger drink with what I have to tell you," said Davis as he giggled.

"Which is?" asked Lon.

"You been married before and I know you married some white gal that you met while you were in the service," said Davis calmly.

"What business is that of yours?" asked Lon angrily.

Kib bumped Lon as he stood at him and rudely said, "We have to know everything about a person when they join us here at Endico Hall. Hell, we know you like them white gals and just keeping in your place if you know what I mean by marrying a Black gal or the lighter side."

"Why is that so important to you?" asked Lon as he was startled by Kib who came out of nowhere.

"We had to know more about you to figure out how you would fit into our establishment," said Kib who demanded another drink.

"So, I was married, and given the situation, we decided to go our separate ways," said Lon as if he were trying to make Kib believe him.

Kib laughed so loud others in the warehouse began to look over at him. "Don't lie to me boy!" yelled Kib.

"Maybe I ought to go!" said Lon as he tried to excuse himself.

"Sit down, you ain't going nowhere," said Kib in a drunken slur.

Lon sat on the edge of his seat and looked Kib directly in the face as Davis stared at them both.

"What else you got to say?" asked Lon.

Well, Elkin said you wanted to use your daughter by way of salvation and that ain't set to right with her cause she carried Drecker for so many months and had horrible childbirth with her as you had to sneak into the hospital to see her because there was still some shame about you a black man being her daddy. You wanted to have your cake and eat it too, but Elkin refused after Drecker was born. She wanted Drecker to have an opportunity in life, she didn't want to be victimized by way of sacrifice for your kinky transgressions or tacky housekeeping you two were into. You enjoyed your sausages and she tried to get you to eat oatmeal and sacrifice. When she told you that you had an ultimatum, you guys had it out and she called the police. and you ran and hid at a friend's house until someone smoothed things over and she demanded that you leave the home or she was going to press charges against you. She had all of your things packed and you temporarily stayed with a friend until you got stationed in a place for you to get a divorce." said Kib who seemed sober for a moment but out of breath from all the talking he was doing.

"Yes, that is true. I have not seen either one of them since. Elkin was a grudge-holding bitch who just wanted me for my body like some of the other women around here. I gave her that and we got married and had a child and then she was done with me. She will use that excuse and make me look bad because she wasn't going to any court to ask for child support from a black man. So is raising Drecker on her own. I can't call her or even contribute financially because according to the terms of the divorce she was going to raise Drecker herself and not ask anything of me. Therefore, I get no visitation rights or say so in her upbringing." said Lon sadly.

"Well, she made a real bitch out of you, and then you went on and got married, and just on the surface you seemed to have settled in," said Lon.

"I don't think it is polite for you to be such a hypocrite but you should consider the fact that we are all in the warehouse for a reason and that is to have some excitement out of life since our wives don't bring us that," said Lon.

"I agree," said Kib.

"Ok, I have had my share of not-so-perfect relationships like the next guy, so why persecute me?" asked Lon. hesitantly.

"Oh, come on Lil, buddy!" said Kib jokingly. "We need you here and we need you to help us with our mission," said Kib.

"I know what your mission is but I'm still trying to figure out how I fit in," asked Lon who seemed confused. "I work and I get paid a decent salary and now I'm on the in-crew with you guys at the warehouse, now what else can a man ask for?" asked Lon

Davis looked at Lon and nodded pathetically. He then asked him, "Man do you like your kids?"

"Sure, I do." smiled Lon as he took out pictures of them when they were babies.

Davis looked at the pictures. "Now I know they are older than that and this is exactly what I'm talking about. They are your kids. You know just for show and you don't know much about them at all because you come to work looking to get in on the in-crowd and then instead of going home of course you slither on in here and get looking to get picked up and shit and you can't even pull out a decent picture of your children."

Lon stared at Davis blankly and he wanted him to shut the fuck up. "Look man, my wife takes all the pictures and she has them. My wallet is heavy enough so I don't need a picture of my kids every year they have to take a new one," said Lon.

"Go on Kib," said Davis.

"We got a real problem with the kids these days. They don't seem to be getting it in school and the teachers have just passed them along to make it look good," said Kib.

"So!" said Lon. "I do not see any problem with that things generally work themselves out when they grow up. They go off to work and get married and have a family of their own. So I don't see what the big deal is and why we have to focus all our energy on our children. Isn't it enough that we bring home our hardworking money and that allows them to have food, clothing, and shelter? We take them on outings like the moves or at least my wife does. These kids these days they got it good and I don't see why we have to try and make scholars out of everyone them in the classroom." said Lon.

"You got that real, I don't care attitude. That must be where Quezel gets it from!" snapped Kib.

Lon got up from his seat and grabbed Kib by the throat. "I would appreciate it if you do not talk about my children or my wife. You do not even know them!"

Davis came from around the bar to break up the scuffle as Kib tried to laugh things off. "You know my wife grabs me between the legs harder than that. Now if you keep on, I will show you what an outdoorsman does and I can mimic the South a whole lot more than you can fake a karate hold." said Kib.

Lon Roner thought to himself. He never wanted to suffer the fate of many southerners who were trapped in an existence of despair and poverty. Many of those people had very little education and minimal skills. If they came up North like many of them did, they would only be relegated to doing housework or working for a family as in being a domestic, chauffeur or groundskeeper just like the homes in the South. He hated to clean, cook, wash or do any tasks that were required to maintain himself. Lon wanted to be part of the group that went to a barber for haircuts and went out for lunch and had extramarital affairs and thought nothing of it. Their kids would sacrifice some to allow this to happen but Lon did seem to mind. Quezel and Teneil were naive, silly, playful, and just fun-loving little girls who wouldn't harm anyone. They were too young to understand the consequences of life and he wanted to keep it that way. The less they knew about things the more he could get away with what he was doing by way of transgression.

"Look, what is it that you're trying to tell me? I'm not sure I follow?" said Lon

Kib took another swig of his drink. "We got them kiddos that got learning issues. They not exactly retards but it ain't getting through," he said.

"Then what are we supposed to do?" asked Lon. "Have them live at home with us?"

"We have a solution," said Kib quietly.

"We gon put the real smart ones like your daughter Teneil with those that are not so smart in the workplace," said Kib proudly as if he thought of something that would revolutionize the world.

Lon laughed at the thought of Teneil going to college and pursuing her dreams and passions and none of it working out because her dear old dad who is an informant for the Klan has to have her work with someone who is learning disabled for the rest of her working life. He giggled at the thought because he often felt guilty for not being there for Drecker. He felt horrible about the way his relationship ended with her mother Elkin. Through Teneil, Lon could release his guilt by having her do his penance for him and making her the butt of the joke. Lon relaxed and even drank a glass of wine. He did not feel bad or guilty anymore. He realized that it was time for him to be who he wanted and do what he wanted to do and for children to be seen and not heard. A woman walked over to him and said, "I'll have what he's having."

"Wine is not too bad," said Lon. "You not too bad looking either." he continued, "But here's the thing, I see your butt over in accounting and you don't look like you do a damn thing. Now is it me or just my imagination?"

"The streets are cold, and I have a service to offer. I didn't see any reason why I could not come into a place like Endico Hall and try things out here. The people are so warm and needy like yourself." said the woman.

"So you are a working girl?" asked Lon.

"This must be your first real job. I usually don't get that question asked too many times." said the woman.

"I've had a few jobs but nothing as business and corporate as this," said Lon.

"My life was rough growing up and I had to make the most of it. I got in here and learned along the way. My working girl experience puts me in the know with a lot of people. Now, I do not have all day. If you're interested I want you to follow me." said the woman as Lon did as she asked.

Chapter Eleven

Teneil watched as her father got ready for work one early Wednesday morning. She heard him talking to her mother Jacel. Lon was grumpy, irritable, and quite nasty. He was slamming things down as usual and acting as if he did not want to be home.

"Please call me if you won't be home at your usual time, the kids get worried," said Jacel as she pleaded with him.

"Those girls ain't worried. They are too busy chatting it up with their classmates. You are the one who likes keeping tabs on me and you want me to call you so that you know what I am doing every moment of the day. I'm sick and tired of this!" snapped Lon.

"What am I doing, that is so wrong in that you seem so distant from us?" asked Jacel.

"Nothing, I'm working, and I have to do what I have to do. I put a decent roof over your head and food on the table and clothes and other things. That takes a lot of money." said Lon.

"You're acting as if I don't contribute by raising our children and working when I can," said Jacel in defense of herself.

"Girl, you don't make enough money to rent a motel room for a month." Laughed Lon. "So how in the world are you going to support us on what you make?"

"Lon, I do what I can in that the money is for extras," said Jacel who was in tears.

Lon put his tie on and giggled. "Extras, like movies and snacks you buy at the supermarket. We got a shit load of junk food lined up in the cabinet that the girls don't eat, and you think you being motherly by buying junk food and giving them an allowance to go out and waste it on nonsense," said Lon.

"No, I think that they would feel deprived if they just had the necessities which are all you seem to bring home. We still have and use most of the things we did when we first got married and it's as if we haven't moved forward and bought our things," said Jacel.

Lon thought to himself as if Jacel was hinting that she wanted a fancier home with all the latest and greatest appliances. "Is that it, you see all of the things we got and still use them but see them as junk and you want to get rid of them. Well, I'm not going to argue there because I don't see it as a necessity. You just want to replace it to have something newer and more expensive. So you go ahead if you want to but don't use the money I have set aside for the mortgage and car and all of the other more important obligations." said Lon.

"So you're watching every penny?" asked Jacel sarcastically.

"Lookey here and I know you ain't no scholar and..." said Lon as Jacel interrupted him.

"Why didn't you marry one?" yelled Jacel.

Lon looked at Jacel and smiled. "Do you think a man wants a walking dictionary and a pocket calculator with him at all times?' asked Lon.

"Well, it would help if you think that the money that you are saving is going to be of use to us in our old age, you're crazier than I thought," said Jacel.

"You spend most of what you make and the little you do put aside because the job you have doesn't provide benefits won't be enough to help us if we both catch colds, so this crap you talking about my not making enough money for the family is a lot of bull and it has to stop. Now, this conversation turned argument you started it because I told you I had to get into the office early, but you want me to be a big daddy to you and I keep telling you we have to focus and make as much money as we can while we are young so that we have enough once we retire," said Lon. "You still act as if before we were married."

"Sometimes I wish we weren't?" said Jacel.

Lon who began to put on his suit jacket wanted to ignore Jacel. She was making a big deal out of things and had to learn to mature and grow up.

"Lon," said Jacel in a soft low voice.

"What?" he asked as he ignored her advances.

"Are you seeing someone for business and that is why you're leaving to go to the office early and coming home later in the evening?" asked Jacel as she looked at him.

Lon tried not to look Jacel in the face because if he did she would know that he was lying and although he doubted she would ever leave him because Jacel loved him in every sense of the word he knew that if he admitted to infidelity even if he were just climbing up the social ladder that she would tell her family and then it would get back to his and make things uncomfortable. There were no saints in Jacel's family and he knew if they said something it would be like throwing stones at a glass house, but there mere fact that they would know his business and how he was working to get there would have them doubt his true capabilities in terms of work. That bothered Lon because then they would say if he were a success that they knew how he got there and he never wanted them to know. Lon wanted to be seen by the world as this intelligent, hardworking individual who put family first and himself last. He didn't want Jacel to ruin that image of him by admitting to infidelity. Lon knew he had to at least pacify Jacel so that she would not talk about this to their family. Lon walked over and hugged Jacel and he whispered. "I love you, but please the office is very demanding and I have to get to work." he said as he grabbed his briefcase and left the house.

Quezel and Teneil look over at each other while lying in bed. "Did you hear that crock of shit?" asked Teneil.

"Yes, I heard them although I couldn't hear everything. But I don't think it was a crock of shit. Dad sounded sincere and mom sounded spoiled as if she wanted his attention as if she were a child." said Quezel.

"It appears as if dad is neglecting his husband's duties if you know what I mean and he is shortchanging us around the house here and making mom go out to work," said Teneil. "He is working more hours and still not bringing home enough money. I find that highly suspicious."

"Not all jobs pay you more when you work late. There's a girl in my class who has a father who works all kinds of hours, and he still does not bring home enough money. You need to get out more. The problem with you is that they put you around affluent kids or kids whose parents are doing well financially. So you don't seem to know anything about the common struggles of the rest of the world." said Quezel.

Teneil thought that it was strange that Quezel could jump out and say those things to her but when it came time for homework she never had an answer other than to say the teacher never assigned her any. Teneil found it strange that her teachers seemed to always have homework and lots of quizzes for her to do as if she were doing homework for two people.

"I think he's up to something because this is not adding up and he seems to have no solid explanation for things," said Teneil.

"Mom's grown, it's her problem so let her handle it!" said Quezel.

"Well, that is the thing. When she questions his whereabouts and becomes insecure, you end up at a friend's house for house and I get two days' worth of homework and have to do your chores. It is just not right," said Teneil.

Quezel knew that Teneil was treated differently because Wendor told her the lay of the land at school. It was a secret that she was made to keep to herself and not tell Teneil and as long as she kept that secret she would be able to get out of doing her homework and other things like chores around the house. This made Quezel happy because she knew she didn't have to do much and could rely on the salvation of Teneil to get over on in life. She knew she could not tell Teneil that her father was part of the ole boy network and everybody had their favorites, and she wasn't one of them.

"Look be thankful you have a place to live and food to eat and clothes to wear," said Quezel. "You're putting pressure to succeed on everyone around you including your parents. Your desire to become makes others do more because they feel as if they are not doing things because of your driven efforts to succeed," said Quezel.

"No hold on a moment, I am not the one who signed up to do double the chores and double the homework and I was given an order, not an option. There's a difference," said Teneil.

"I do my part also as I assist others on the outside. I am loving and caring, so sometimes I cannot be home because I help out elsewhere," said Quezel.

"Charity starts at home and you need to understand that," yelled Teneil.

"I will do as I please, if I want to help the less fortunate I will do so. If I see a friend or someone in need and I can be of assistance I will do as I please," said Quezel angrily. She did not want to listen to Teneil because of the pact that she made with Wendor at school. She knew that she was not good in school and Wendor told her that she didn't have to be good in school all she had to do was follow along with the way they planned things, and all would be ok.

"Ok, we're different, but there were times that I wished you helped out more," said Teneil sadly.

"We all have our crosses to bear and I cannot help you with what you have to do on your own," said Quezel who turned over and decided to go back to sleep.

"It's time to get ready for school," said Teneil.

"You usually go first and I won't be walking with you because I have something to do with Wendor and her mom is giving us a ride. Now you get going because you don't want to be late," said Quezel.

Teneil got up out of bed and went to shower and she thought to herself tearfully as the water flowed. It must be that Kib Drendel that's making a bad influence on everyone. Dad's leaving the house early and comes home late and Quezel never does homework and would rather spend time with other people than with her sister. She knew she had to find out more and she did not want to ask her mother because she knew that if she did she would just give her more chores to do.

Teneil was coming out of the bathroom and her mother Jacel said, "Good now as I am getting ready you can clean the dishes out of the dishwasher and take the meat out of the freezer and put it in the fridge to thaw out." she said.

"Couldn't Quezel do that?" she asked.

"She says she does not feel well. I may have to take her to the doctor, and she said that you were giving her a hard time. I do not understand you, Teneil. How would you like it if someone was bothering you if you were sick?" her mother asked.

"That's not what she told me," said Teneil.

"She says she does not like to tell you anything because you don't understand her and that is not good Teneil." said Jacel.

"I suppose I can never get sick with the way you work me around here," said Teneil as she walked into her room.

"Don't try to get out of doing things by saying that you are..." said Jacel, "And don't wake Quezel either."

"This is exactly what I mean," mumbled Teneil.

Chapter Twelve

"Yes Mr. Deivers we're working on it, but these kids don't seem too friendly," said Principal Marshman.

"I understand you have a graduation coming up in a few days and Quezel is going to be getting most of the awards. We can't give them to others because well we cannot give awards to certain ones as a reputation. But your real reason for contacting me is to keep an eye on Teneil. She has numerous capabilities but we need to put her at the heart of it all for this to be effective. I do not see her as voluntarily wanting to go South to do this. if you know what I mean. As things move towards technology it's a grim feeling that our schools will be overcrowded with children who have problems that are noticeable and your classrooms will be as empty as the notebooks my students come in with," said Mr. Deivers.

"The good thing is that Quezel and Teneil will not be my problem anymore. Now I got my yella wonder doling out the awards for the graduation. Ain't nobody gon fuck with her ass or argue fairness because she can keep those brownies in line. Now her great-grandfather was out there so to speak and had a thing for them, but he was a hell of a klansman. Anyways, he had the idea to be techy about things since we couldn't chain em' to the fields. He began to notice that some of them brownies were very smart and could be useful because seeming to me some of the wives were the dumbest of what existed and it was as if they always needed help doing everything but sex. But hey that was the man's job so them women did nothing much at all. Anyways, he dun come up with the idea to have the real smart brownies assist our kind." said Principal Marshman.

"I do see this as a good investment because it salvages our reputation because we can then use people like Teneil for our efforts to continue with superiority," said Mr. Deivers.

"Did you say investment?" asked Principal Marshman.

"Yes, investment!" said Mr. Deivers.

"Look, you are our Jewish informant. You wanted to be down with us and you signed up for it so that we don't oust you and have you hanging with your own and some of the brownies," said Principal Marshman angrily.

"If you can't beat em' you join em' and that's the way I was looking at things. My religion came down hard after all of your supremacy and I couldn't go on no more. So I sold out but it was only so that I didn't have to fear the same problem here in America. Y'all do no work but you about the business when it comes to giving it to others. Now, I'm sure there will be others like Teneil and I will do my best to have all of these people assist those who are learning challenged and who do not fit into our school curriculum because they can speak and outwardly they look normal. But as far as other things go they need some assistance. So please leave my family be and I will do as you ask." said Mr. Deivers.

"I think we will have a wonderful partnership and as you get more involved you have as much to lose as the rest of us if this gets exposed. So don't think of any funnies if you suddenly decide you want or get a bleeding heart over some brownie you don't want to burn." said Principal Marshman.

"But this is so much on a person so young. I'm in favor of all of this but they have to be trained to handle all that we are going to put at them. I understand that her father Lon is helping us with all of this because he like me is an informant but Teneil is just too small and delicate and I was just wondering if there was something else we could do." said Mr. Deivers.

"No tears. That is a sign of weakness and if you show weakness for them what will you do for your own?" asked Principal Marshman.

Mr. Deivers did not want to go there with Principal Marshman. He was a rough bigot who normally hired the ole yella kind to beat and punish the kids in the Catholic sense and equip them with a lack of motivation and skill set so that they would never finish high school. Principal Marshman knew that when you needed a brownie to do something you had to start them young. That meant getting them in trouble so that their parents would beat them and adding on extra homework so that when the accreditation board came around and they crunched the numbers and played with the books it would appear as though Houses Elementary School was on top of things. But truthfully, they were not. They were a shell of an old schoolhouse that was planted North. The textbooks were for preschoolers and of course for those like Teneil they would give work that was two grades higher. She would cry because when she got home she had other things to do but life here in the suburbs was different. Teneil was about to learn how it was to live in the South.

"Ok, Teneil will learn the struggle as it is a legacy of what makes a culture of people," said Mr. Deivers.

"That's what I want to hear because I'm putting this in your hands as I get ready for the next school season and more new challenges," said Principal Marshman.

A few days passed and Quezel and Wendor were graduating from sixth grade.

"See girl, I told you," said Wendor. "Now if you just play by the rules you get out of doing that boring stuff like homework and get to hang out all day. You're getting awards just like I am. You see, they favor the superior look." said Wendor.

Quezel was happy but she felt slightly guilty because Teneil had been transferred to a school on the southside of town. After all, her capabilities had to be enlightened so that she would be able to do all that was expected of her. Quezel knew she, herself was lazy and not the smartest but she just wanted to help her little sister but she didn't know how.

Principal Marshman and the biggin herself Valdena Plantation presented the awards to a few students most of who were light in color and a few dark-skinned people, but it was a very biased graduation. Teneil knew something was off because she did not see Quezel do the homework it would take to garner all of the awards she earned but it was one of those things that she had already figured out and knew that it was accepted among those in the burbs because this is what they had to tolerate to live here. When people complained they would always tell them that it was worse in the South and if they were not happy they could go there if they choose to. Lon stood quietly and proudly as Wendor's father Kib kept his family away from Lon's. They acknowledged each other briefly but that was it. Teneil noticed this and thought to herself, "That man works where her father does and Quezel is known to go by Wendor's house and Kib looked as unfriendly as a ghost in a stadium." she said herself. Two white women walked over and hugged Wendor and chatted it up with her and her family. Lon watched them and went into a daze of envy.

He admired the white women and if it wasn't for his fear of being singled out as the black one he would have remained married to his first wife. But he knew as long as he had his complexion and they had theirs there would always be a difference. Bren Chopper's brother had received a few awards and walked over and congratulated Quezel, as Bren smiled and waved at Teneil.

"Fuck is your mother fucking problem!" snapped Lon.

"Pardon?" asked Mr. Chopper.

"You just walked over bumped into me and did not apologize and kept going. Hell is wrong with you?" Lon yelled.

It was crowded outside but Mr. Chopper certainly didn't bump Lon Roner so he didn't need to apologize. "I didn't bump into you but if I did I am certainly sorry," said Mr. Chopper.

People watched as the graduation took a sour note and Lon Roner became ghetto. "Oh now you're sorry!" said Lon.

"What else do you want?" asked Mr. Chopper.

Lon grabs Mr. Chopper and punches him to the ground as people watch in horror and go to break up the fight.

It took several people to subdue Lon and then several other people including another white woman walked over to Mr. Chopper and took a wet cloth and put it over his face.

"Man, was that necessary?" yelled another man from a distance. You can't be from the South, you got no fortitude to suck up even the smallest things. Who's handling your clear for you because you can't seem to be doing this yourself, dang you stupid. Beautiful day out, the kids are all healthy and you ticked a bitch with a pickle up your butt cause you trying to be incognito about shit. I know you and you don't scare me or fool me either." said the man who appeared to be from another planet.

"You want your ass beat too?" asked Lon.

"I'm going to take a rain check on this one but we gon meet again and I'm gon have something for that ass!" said the man. "Enjoy your day," he said as he walked off with what appeared to be his girlfriend.

Lon thought quickly as the man seemed to know him but Lon didn't recognize him in any of his travels. He cooled off as Bren waved silently to Teneil and she waved back and several people helped them to their car. "I take it you know him?" asked Lon as he looked at Teneil.

"Know who?" asked Teneil.

"The boy you were waiving to!" snapped Lon.

"Oh, the one whose father you gave your formal introduction to?" asked Teneil as her mother Jacel laughed helplessly.

"The guy was rude and had no sense about himself. I mean Black people have got to get it together!" yelled Lon.

Jacel looked around, "Where's Quezel she was here a moment ago?" she asked.

"I will go find her," said Teneil as she knew that her father hit Mr. Chopper on purpose because they were in a heated battle over being the house negro. Teneil knew her father hated black people and would often conspire against them so that he could be the only one. He knew if he integrated he would be in a place where they have laws and protection against work abuse and if he played the role he could have his way and do a lot less than the others. He punched Mr. Chopper on purpose so that they would take the disruption out on her at her graduation. Teneil knew she had her work cut out for her as her parents always made sure she did the family penance and tithe along the way.

"Babe," said the woman as they sat in her car." Did you know that man, you were putting the mouth on?" she asked.

"I know of him." said the man as he smoked a cigarette.

"How you know of him, he kinda older than us?" asked the woman.

"He was in the Navy with my Uncle Razel and Razel talked about him all the time." said the man. "He didn't like him very much and he knew all of his dirty secrets."

"Just like I know yours, Big Troy." said the woman.

Big Troy grabbed the woman and kissed her.

Chapter Thirteen

Mary Weedham had finally been going over the accounts at Trinity Health Insurance Company. She was not happy. There seemed to be more money going out than going in. "But how could this be?" she thought to herself. The company had a checklist of measures put into place so that they know when to deny or approve a service. Mary went to retrieve the paper checklist forms that were supposed to be stored on a micro disk, but they were not there. Numaar Insurance Company had gone through a change including a name change to Trinity Health Insurance Company and now that the letters were being done by computer and all the transcriptionists would have to do is to check the patient demographics in the system and then take the medical decision that was semi-automated according to the guidelines and construct the letter. The problem with the letters was that the format was changing constantly due to the demands of the state and Trinity Health Insurance Company had to upgrade its software to meet the demands of the state. Mary knew it would be too late to send letters of overpayment to hospitals and facilities because if she were to do that they would know that Trinity Health Insurance Company was not up to the task of its bookkeeping. Mary knew they have six years of a look-back period to recoup payments, "But what if these companies changed hands or were out of business altogether?" she said as she know she would need help in locating all of the files to do a complete six-year audit. Stace had been with the company for several years so Mary decided to ask Stace to help her. Perhaps Stace would know why many of the letters were approved.

"Hey, Stace?" said Mary over the phone.

"Yes," said Stace who was curious about why Mary was calling her.

"Could you come here a moment, I need to ask you something?" said Mary who tried not to sound too worried.

"I'll be right there," said Stace.

Stace completed her letter and then walked over to the accounting area in the business department and found Mary looking at her computer screen.

"Hi, Mary." She said happily. "What did you need?"

"Mary looked up and said, "Trinity Health Insurance Company is in huge financial trouble, and we need to gather our resources to get out from under otherwise we will be going out of business.

Stace remained calm knowing that the approval letters that were being done had made a huge dent in the overall financial health and survival of the company. Stace knew that for years when the company was called Numaar and was making a profit they never shared the wealth with the company. They would hand out gift certificates and always make it sound like they were always in the red and were going to stay that way. They never had a problem with the State and Stace wondered if this was the reason Mary was calling her.

"We ran into a problem?" said Mary.

"What?" asked Stace.

"Our checks are bouncing, and we had to go into our reserve money. A vendor we often used complained to the State about not being paid for services that he rendered to our members. The man bitched and stated that if he didn't get his money within 60 days he was going to sue us and stop doing business with us." said Mary.

"Are checks bouncing with other vendors?" asked Stace.

"Yes, but we have a lot of vendors who enjoy working with us and they are patient while we work to straighten things out. But, if we start making staff suffer by delaying their paychecks or even having to trim staff down this will cause a problem in the productivity of our work," said Mary.

"Well, what do you want from me?" asked Stace.

"I need you to find the checklist for each letter for the past six years so that we can determine if everything was sent out correctly so that we can establish if we need to send out letters requesting that the overpayment be returned."

Stacy began to feel nervous but she wasn't going to let Mary get to her. She had been doing this long enough to know that companies go out of business, merge, and after a while, you spend more money trying to recoup payments than you do in receiving them. Sometimes it's easier to write off the debt as a loss rather than to go after it. But in doing so the State would come in and mention that they do not have enough of a reserve to stay in business and give them a certain amount of time to improve their financial status. If they don't do it within a certain amount of time the State could make them close their doors or the State could have them bought out to a competitor.

"That's a lot of work for me to do and six years ago we were still on paper and we store all of the old work in a warehouse, but do you remember the storm?" asked Stace.

"How could I forget? We had to close the building for several days and that was when Numaar decided to automate." said Mary.

"Stace thought about how her workers were diligent enough to remove those letters that they had sent to providers giving them approval once they were paid. Then she thought perhaps if they were to match up every approved letter with a paid claim she knew they would be in trouble. Stace knew she had to act quickly to find somebody to help her so that there would be no way to locate the bogus claims that were paid out.

"You want me to find the old letters and checklists in the warehouse," said Stace.

"That's a start, and that's all we have to go on for now. We took quite a beating with the storm. But if the providers don't pay us within 60 days there will be a penalty of interest added on to what they owe and I'm sure that were can be up to date enough for the State not to make us close our doors." said Mary.

Stace knew that there were errors in payments not only due to her bogus work but because sometimes a claim was so complicated Numaar just paid at the contracted rate because it took too long to manually search out every contract and look up every time to see if it were paying correctly. People who worked at Trinity Health Insurance Company were not the brightest and it wasn't a wise idea to just box up everything and put it into storage because the warehouses were not waterproof. After all, the property needed work and so did the buildings on it. Numaar Insurance was cheap and now that it became Trinity Health Insurance Company they didn't want to pay to have documents stored on films or microfiche. They didn't want to pay someone to scan the documents and maintain several microfiche readers on the premises because it would require a team of workers and it would not be cost-effective since the microfiche reader would not be used very often. By storing things in boxes and storage units and cataloging them, it would be easier to locate the original documents. The storm saved her because a lot of the original information was ruined and unreadable.

"I think there's a guy named Tang that heads up the department. I will talk to him. But this is going to take some time and my supervisor will still expect me to do my job." said Stace.

"I need you to see to it that Tang has his workers bring the records to me and I will try and match these up claim for a claim," said Benita.

"But what if you find errors done by people who no longer work here, then what?" asked Stace.

"I will just have people from claims correct the error." said Mary, "While they are doing that, once an overpayment is determined I need you to send out the letters. As we become more automated as a whole we can keep an accurate record of what money we have. I thought we were doing quite well until we began to get calls and for some reason, we thought we had more money to pay for everything but it seems as though we do not."

"Is there going to be a formal announcement of sorts to the company or as we going to keep this between us? I know things will get out because you have claims matching up every letter with all of the claims that were paid this is going to be quite daunting. They will be taking each claim per member to see if everything was paid accurately." said Mary.

"What if we don't find records of all of those claims?" asked Stace curiously.

"We will identify those claims and then ask those providers to provide proof that the paid claim was valid by requesting the approval letter. If they cannot produce the letter we will request an overpayment to be returned to us," said Mary. "As far as a formal announcement there will be one of those loudspeaker conferences that will tell everyone to continue working as they normally do and to do the due diligence in making sure that each claim is paid correctly and each letter is approved by supporting documentation," said Mary.

Stace was getting used to making money on the side and she was about to save and do other things that she would have not been able to do by working just for Trinity Health Insurance Company. She hated the thought of giving all of this up and had to find a way of creating bogus checklists for a service to be approved with a doctor's signature. "I will get in touch with Tang as soon as I get back to my desk." said Stace.

"Thanks," said Mary.

Stace went back to her desk and thought for a moment. The authorization numbers were generated in batches and one of her contacts had given her a supply of authorizations to use for the bogus letters. She just hoped that Devou was not approached by anyone about the authorization numbers that were used for claims that were paid out as a result." Stace knew it would be a simpler process to gather the authorizations and go through them. But due to the storm, they were no longer in any order. She remembered Devou using this time to put them out of order so that no one would be able to trace what authorizations were bogus or not because everything was out of sequence.

Stace grabbed her cell phone and called Benita and then Devou. "Hey guys," she said cheerfully.

"Oh, no girl you did not put me on a three-way. You know what underwear I wear when we do it like this," he said jokingly.

Benita laughed. "Look I haven't taken lunch yet. Where are you going?" she asked.

"I want you both to come with me we have some things to discuss," said Stace.

"Ok, I'll be there in a few, I got to get to the boy's room to straighten out my girls." said Devou.

"I'm on my way!" said Benita.

Stace wanted to hold a brief meeting outdoors so that she could convince everyone to continue doing what they were doing. She didn't want to stop her bogus letter business because that would be less income for herself and her family. It had to keep going. There was no choice, if they stopped with companies merging and not accepting certain health insurances it would be a disaster for many private pay companies knowing that they may not agree to the single case agreement payouts. She logged off of her computer and walked out and saw Devou and Benita.

Chapter Fourteen

Lessy sees Lon Roner in a newly renovated cafeteria after the ACTS merger with AUXY. Everything had pretty much stayed the same except they were a larger company. Lon hated mergers because it meant that you were not in contact with the day-to-day people at the top. This also meant that if he wanted to meet someone, they may want him to befriend someone to who he wasn't attracted. Lon knew he would get angry and have to use Teneil as a bargain to get what he wanted. He had a younger son named Lon Jr. who was having issues but Jacel seems as though she was helping him although he was not in grade school yet. Lon had already been in contact with Mr. Deivers and they felt it appropriate to get him started on speech and other things like memory or retention because when children can't retain things they do poorly in school and the workplace because they cease to remember how to do things and would always need help in doing a task. He wondered if these problems with what they call autism were related to dementia in many ways. Lon was just finishing some baked salmon when she approached him.

"Hey Lon," she said quietly.

"Hey Lessy, how's it going?" asked Lon.

"I should be asking you that?" she said as she giggled.

"Hell, you mean by that?" asked Lon defensively.

"You never talk about her, but we know you have an ex-wife and you paying the dirty deed for marrying a white woman," said Lessy.

"Well, I didn't put that on my job application so how do you know my business?" asked Lon curiously.

"I got friends all over the place and I know that you been wiring money like you hot wiring a car or something and then you go over to one of them payphones and talk until lunchtime is over. So I say to myself, it ain't like you got grown kids living in another state or other family that you want to make sure they make ends meet because you don't seem to talk about any. Then I say to myself, he must get another woman, and then from what my sources tell me that's exactly what it is." said Lessy.

"Like you don't have a past?" asked Lon.

"Let's just say yours is more interesting and when it comes to wiring money, I say that there are children involved," said Lessy.

"Yes, you are correct," said Lon reluctantly.

"By the amount of money that you are sending it's probably just one child unless your children are anorexic. Now, I hear you got more children by another wife and the second wife does not know about the first wife because you like to keep it pure at home so that your neighbors don't think you putting out seed as a landscaper does," said Lessy.

"Speaking of gardens, I hear you do a lot of backyard work!" laughed Lon.

"Look, I think we can help each other out," said Lessy.

"I don't think you need any help in the caboose department. But rumor has it that you had a husband named Big Troy and he just up and left you. Now, if you open ass for every man that walks through the revolving door I see why he got a little pissed." said Lon.

"It wasn't like that when we were together," said Lessy tearfully.

"So you were his loyal woman until he up and left you?" asked Lon.

"Yes!" said Lessy painfully. "I don't understand it and I never will."

"Did you call the authorities?" asked Lon.

"Man please, they ain't no help. I mean they searched the hospitals, parks, rivers, homeless shelters, and abandoned cars and places like that and even wooded areas and homes that are not occupied but they did not find anything and without a body of sorts that think that he may have disappeared on his own free will," said Lessy.

"Did you try his family and did you get along with them?" asked Lon.

Lessy sat and thought about how she tried to bond with her in-law's family. It wasn't easy at first but she was getting the hang of things and then once this happened Big Troy just disappeared on her. "They never answer or return my phone calls."

"I think he may be staying with family," said Lon.

"I think so too, and I have even rented cars and did a drive-by to kind of roll up on him and These are no signs of him anywhere. I see his family come and go as if nothing has changed and no phone call as to if they ever heard anything from the police," said Lessy as she wiped her eyes.

"Is this what's making you suspicious, in that they seem to be very calm and act as though nothing is going on," said Lessy. "That is what makes me so suspicious."

"Have you tried hiring a private detective?" asked Lon.

"Well, I been trying to hire one by using my caboose but the detective wouldn't take the job because if I was willing to conduct business in this manner he would know that I didn't keep a clean home and if I didn't keep a clean home then that would be why Big Troy left me. So now we're back to square one," said Lessy.

Lon gave in and decided to help Lessy out. She was pathetic and pouring her heart out to him. "Come on Lessy you have children to take care of and you got to keep it together. Who knows, maybe he got some kind of past that he had to go back to and that's where he went," said Lon.

"But he told me everything and we were together for several years," said Lessy who seemed to have a problem with letting Big Troy go.

"There is a new guy on board at AUXY who worked as a private detective at one point I will talk to him and ask if he knows anybody who can do such a favor for you. But my way of thinking on this is that Big Troy may be in jail and his family is too ashamed to talk with you about it because depending on the nature of the crime they don't want to reveal any information that may make him found guilty," said Lon.

Lessy smiled because that was the one place that she didn't check or even think to ask the police about. When she met Big Troy she knew he had been in jail a few times but it was never anything too serious or something that put him away for more than a year. Why didn't she think of this before? Lessy became angry because she knew Big Troy was street and so was, she which is why they made such a good couple or so she thought. It had been several years and if his past had caught up with him, he could be jailed in another town or even another state.

"So, when are you going to the warehouse again?" asked Lessy anxiously.

"Towards the end of the week. I will ask him then or see if I see him around," said Lon.

"Good. I want closure or..." said Lessy as she did not finish her sentence.

"Girl, you just want him back and you giving away the store to fill your void and loneliness. You have to make your life mean more than just a lay with some third-party business associate," said Lon.

"I didn't come by my education on a Rhodes Scholarship. I had to hit the pavement and do the get to know to get where I wanted to be. So if that meant giving up the peephole to cover the cost of overhead for a joint such as AUXY then so be it and I say we're in business. Besides Big Troy did his thang out there but he always came back to me. Then he wasn't around, and I needed ends and scraps that Troy would provide for me and he wasn't there for me so I was left with mouths to feed and I did what a girl must do." said Lessy as she began to feel proud of herself.

"Somethings gotta change," said Lon.

"Is that how you got out of paying child support, you just came up with an amount and wired it to Elkin?" asked Lessy.

"How did you know her name?" asked Lon.

Lessy laughed. "Boy, you're more of a mess than I thought. When you were sending your wired money through and using your money order to do so you had put the carbon piece of it in the garbage. One day the garbage was so full but you were trying to get rid of it that you threw it in there anyway and I saw you do it as you walked away carelessly. I picked up the carbon piece of paper and saw Elkin Khann on it so I knew you had some business outside of your marriage that you were handling. You think you are so slick you got on out of the marriage cause you knew no law was going to stop their hate towards people. You knew the courts would mess you up something awful and probably find a reason to throw you in jail. She didn't want that for you and you didn't want that for yourself, so you agreed to wire things so that you don't hear a sound from her and the police don't come along hot-wiring your ass because of all the money you should be paying out. Now, what gets me is that with the present thang you have." said Lessy.

"She's called a wife," said Lon, you used to be one you know.

"Stop the chatter. I am talking here. You gave her a batch of kids and you run around the warehouse playing hoops with these other women. It seems like nothing satisfies you. Now, what if you make another baby that ain't your color-breed? You gon wire the baby mama the money also?" asked Lessy.

"I'm hoping I don't have to make that decision again," said Lon as he tried to sound intelligent.

"You know these women at some point are looking to be taken care of. You keep going like a three-wheeled tricycle one of these women gon get you to marry them and you may have to leave town to take care of them," said Lessy.

"I think I am done with children. These women know what they are getting themselves into so I'm not going to allow some woman to pressure me into marrying them because I knocked them up. You see the way they go around here. Anybody could be the father, so I'm not going to be put off by some other woman's nonsense," said Lon.

Elkin Khann watched Drecker as she played outdoors with her younger sister. She was newly divorced and was still in love with Lon and she wanted to rekindle their relationship. Perhaps she could find a way to contact Lon or introduce herself to Jacel and find a way to be one big happy family. Elkin thought of how to do this without letting on that she wanted Lon back into her life. She decided to contact Lon and make him aware that she wanted Drecker to be in his life again. This would not remove the money he had to pay her, but it would of course allow him to see his daughter and give Elkin a way to see Lon as well. Elkin was given enough money in her divorce settlement to stay at home at least for a while but she knew eventually she had to go back to work. She looked in the paper and saw a job advertisement for AUXY. "Hmm, maybe I will apply for a job there. I know this is something that I am capable of doing," she said.

Chapter Fifteen

"Look, I know that you think these kids are too young, but we need to get them started now," said Kib Drendel as he stared out of a hotel room window.

The man named Kel Harper stood silent almost to the point of nausea. He then struggled as he began to speak. "I just didn't want to have to involve my kids in this KKK business so early. We segregate them as much as we can and the colored don't exactly give up, we move and they follow us. They come into the school system and learn what our kids learn. " said Kel as he smoked a cigarette.

"That's why in certain school districts we dummy the work down." laughed Kib. "If you think we gon make scholars out of these people you got another thing coming."

"Then why teach if you're not going to do the work involved?" said Kel with a frown. "If the teachers are not motivated to teach and they are turned off by who they have to teach then they should just go someplace else."

"No, my boy," said Kib as he drank some bourbon out of a bottle. "Ain't but so many places to teach and you can't fit all of them into one place. So what we like to do is to take the worst of them and put them into school districts with many minorities. We got problems with joblessness, crime, drugs, and broken households so when many of these kids come to school they barely got their homework done cause they are too preoccupied with the other things they got going on and many of them only get to a certain grade level before they end up dropping out. So where does that lead their future?" asked Kib.

"That's my point," said Kel.

"Your point," said Kib as he moved away from the window.

"These kids are broken with very few resources designed to put them in the right direction. Many of them will go onto low-paying jobs and have kids or families of their own. They are not a threat to us so our mission of maintaining superiority and authority will hold no matter what." said Kel. "So why do we bother with the few that are out there?" he asked.

"Because they breed and the more they breed the more they will make to go on and do certain things that they can do. Many of these people create a way to get by for themselves that enables them to live like privileged people. We have to control the future and the population of this,..." said Kib.

"We can have certain masses sacrifice for them," said Kel.

"That's what we're going to talk about," said Kib as he heard a knock on the door. Kib got up and looked and there was several members of the Klan walking in the door with either a beer bottle or whiskey and smoking cigarettes.

"What's the meeting going to be about today." asked one man as he sat on the edge of the bed.

"It has come to our attention that people are using talent instead of education to make it in this world and if so we will not be able to oppress the masses if this occurs," said Kib

"You mean like this rap music nonsense that the kids are doing?" asked the man.

"Exactly. These kids and grown adults are finding a niche in the entertainment industry and those who would normally be out selling for the man have found a way to entertain and make money by doing it. This helps out a lot of inner-city people who need money to support themselves." said Kib.

"Well, we can have our kids start doing the same thing." said another man.

"It's frightening." said Kib rather loudly. "That a bunch of kids took something and created music out of it, like thin air. It's a threat because more and more kids are doing it and this gets them out of poverty and then of course you find them living in our neighborhoods and..."

"Dating our people!" laughed the man because now they have the money to afford such a lifestyle and to take care of the costs involved to live in a superior race.

"You know these artists spend more to fit into our race of people. They just don't marry the wife they marry the entire family and end up supporting the entire family so it's not like they gon just go out and buy mama shit cause they got to appease the mother-in-law and her side of the family also. That's some slavery shit right there boy. Imagine you get a record deal and you think you going to support or give money to your siblings, mama, grandma, or whoever raised you and then you meet a woman, and cause she's white you got to take her to all of the fancy restaurants and buy her clothes and all kinds of jewelry. Having a woman out of your normal class of folk will cost you. Now, the record companies ain't no fool, they kind of make it so that the money they make doesn't go to their own." said the man. "So if they are not able to do too much with the money they spend but to give it back to the man then our point is mute."

The rest of the Klux Association began to walk toward the man and one of them punched him.

The man bent over in pain. "You didn't have to do that." the man said. "I ain't of no harm and I didn't say anything thing out of the ordinary. It's the truth you seem to think that this white world of ours is going to let every highly successful individual just up and earn whatever they want without paying for it in some way or another. This country ain't like that." yelled the man named Raul.

"And we want to keep it that way." he offered the man a sip of bourbon. "Our mission is to remove the foundation of our forefathers from them so that they have to create their own," said Kib.

Raul was holding his side and still bent over. "But we gotta keep doing this for every damn generation that comes along. We can't rest," said Raul angrily.

"And they not going to either." laughed Kib. "See if we just say ok, you paid your dues then they will create future generations that will walk the earth without as much of a sacrifice and what would that say for our freedoms? If they don't pay then at some point we will because they will keep their own money and it will never become ours. In enslavement, they sign everything over and of course, we give them something to make them work, such as a white woman because they may not want to put the effort into it if it were otherwise. We give them what we don't want and then they work just to give the money back to us. Now if that ain't a commodity I don't know what is." said Kib as the others agreed.

"So you think I'm going soft?" asked Raul.

"I know you best ta get it together." said Kib." Now we have to talk to our fellow brotherhood and let it be known that for every artist's success and I mean success in that they live like some wealthy white, that's a threat and others must sacrifice to see that person in stardom so to speak. Now, this is going to be a way to control the population of success and to have just regular workers toiling around working and doing the jobs they should be doing.

"How do we find out who is up and coming?" asked Raul as he lay on the bed slightly out of it.

"We got ourselves and an informant and we're going to need more of them. A guy named Lon Roner who works at AUXY with me has been quite a guy. He knows many of the minorities and what these children are up to and he reports back to me if he feels as though they are going to make it within the context of our forefather foundation. Like I said before we can't have people just out and going to school and getting a high-paid job. Too easy, we want some foundation creation before we do that." said Kib.

"Yup, that's how you know the difference between a child of God or the slave of man," said Raul. "I completely understand you but at the same time aren't you worried about the repercussions that we may subject ourselves to religiously?"

"Then the LORD said to him, "Know for certain that for four hundred years your descendants will be strangers in a country not their own and that they will be enslaved and mistreated there., that was taken from Genesis 15:13 NIV." said Kib. "Now what we do is every time a new job, merger, or takeover begins a new 400-year or treatment begins. As far as our need to stay superior we found a discrepancy that we used in oppressive treatment. They called them Jim Crow Laws but it was a biblical discrepancy that we choose to take advantage of, 'Now the length of time the Israelite people lived in Egypt was 430 years.', that was taken from Exodus 12:40."

"So you're saying that the Israelites were slaves for actually 400 years and that Jim Crow laws with the minstrel shows that began in the 1830's were established to extend the treatment of blacks for thirty years more?" asked Raul.

Kib smiled. "Now you see why biblically if someone is paying restitution outside of a jail cell we pad the slave time to it by using Exodus 12:40 instead of Genesis 15:13. Because it was Exodus we had to leave from the beginning so to speak and move towards the end of the whole thing but that didn't mean we could enslave them any less as times were changing due to the minstrel of Jim Crow."

"So you want us to go by Exodus 12:40, when we do this?" asked Raul.

"Yes, the study of polytheism is the study of having more than one God or as in ruler of men. The Israelites only believed in one God. So, we gon Jim Crow it until they become a child of God or the slave of man." said Kib.

"So where do people like Lon Roner come into play?" asked Raul.

"As if you didn't know we have a few on the house as in-house negro. We can only have a few and then the rest must sacrifice. We will

thwart the efforts of most to keep enslavement during these modern
times very much alive." said Kib.

"Let the best God win!" said Raul as he got up.

"Meeting adjourned," said Kib. as the men shook hands and patted
each other on the backs.

Latrel had quietly entered the adjourning hotel room and was
listening to the conversation. She had to find out who Lon Roner was
and spread the word that he was an informant. What she had going
with Kib was to keep her job at a nearby factory and as long as she
was able to do that, she could support her children. She knew that Kib
worked for AUXY and there were many employees there. She decided
not to ask him much. Instead, she would focus on AUXY and ask
around. It bothered her that Lon Roner wanted to be the house negro
and would throw others under the bus. The door to her room was
closed as she would normally open it, but she didn't want him to know
she was there all along waiting for him. She found a phone book and
looked Lon up and copied down his address. She decided to ask a few
friends to find out more about him. He had to be stopped. If people
like Lon Roner continued to do the things they do black women would
be bed-winches forever and black men would always be bankrupt and
emasculated. Everyone had left the hotel room and Kib quickly jumped
in and out of the shower and opened the adjoining door. He knocked a
few times and then he knocked again. Kib smiled as he looked at Latrel,
"Now, you not any work at all!" he said.

Chapter Sixteen

A woman from Caid-Care sat in her office and looked over the year payments that they made to the Trinity Health Insurance Company. She knew that it took years to catch up to companies who bilk the system, but this was ridiculous. Trinity Health Insurance company had been ripping off Caid-Care for at least ten years and nobody noticed. "How could this be?" asked Karlotta Sampton. She went through piles and piles of papers of services that were approved and noticed that there was an unusual amount. Even if services were approved for many visits the services were stretched out so that a member would still be accommodated but without as many hours of assistance. Karlotta looked at many recent statements and said, "I'm gon find the culprit who probably drives a fancy car, puts their kids in private schools, and lives in one of them fancy glass houses." she said to herself knowing that the average salary at Trinity Health Insurance Company was not enough to live off of. Karlotta realized that this was one scheme of many for Trinity Health Insurance. Karlotta then realized that Caid-Care was billed as secondary insurance for all of the services that were approved and if you are covered under Trinity Health Insurance then that plan would take the place of Caid-Care, But the problem was that Trinity in its thirst to attract new members and to continue with its existing membership left out many of the details about what they covered. Trinity would make it seem like they were this robust insurance-managed care plan taking over the world to create the first-of-its-kind socialized medicine conglomerate. They would encourage new membership by promising medical care as if it were private insurance. Members would find themselves going to health clinics, and hospitals and seeing the usual types of doctors in disadvantaged neighborhoods who normally accepted Caid-Care. But billing Caid-Care as a secondary was a no-no with managed care and Trinity Health Insurance Company had some explaining to do if they thought that this was a way to handle business legally. Many of the payments made to Trinity were going to a post office box that was not designated to send legitimate payments. She contacted Hal Kesker who was part of the investigation unit at Caid-Care so that she could have his team do a full investigation because this would mean that many facilities were being paid twice. She wondered how much people were making at Trinity Health Insurance who falsified the approval letters so that they could collect money from the facility, provider, or hospital. The phone continued to ring as Hal Kasker picked up.

"Hal Kesker, what can I do for you?" he asked

"Hey Hal, it is Karlotta. I need your expertise on this one," said Karlotta.

"What seems to be going on that you have to interrupt me in the middle of my golf game? We called it quits years ago." Hal yelled.

"The problem was that little putter of yours," said Karlotta calmly. "You couldn't feed a bird and I'm not the only one who has had that experience, so I don't think I'm spilling tee here."

"Said the bottom-heavy woman with more cracks and crevices than a mountain." laughed Hal. "I heard you once went on a double date and because your bottom was so heavy the two guys never met each other."

Karlotta tried to remain calm, but Hal tried her patience at times. "Listen Hal we have had our disagreements, but I do not think you should be bitter over the fact that hair strands can go deeper than you. You are taking this way too far and became upset at the fact that you didn't want to use your health insurance to become a big guy and compete with the other fellas. You are cheap!" snarled Karlotta.

"Do you know what people at the job will think if I start trying to grow my manhood, now?" asked Hal.

"What?" asked Karlotta.

"It would be as if I neglected to pay attention to all of this. I tried out of pocket, but you must understand all of this is costly and I still have to put a roof over my head. so this whole thing of wanting to make myself transparent just to give you a good time when you want one is highly unnecessary." yelled Hal. "Now I have a girl who loves and respects me now and we have a ball together and you're calling me because you're jealous and trying to break things up between us."

Karlotta shook her head. "I happen to know that you adopted a daughter about a year ago because your sperm needs a bus ride to fertilize anything. I mean this is awful having your sperm too tired to do anything once it gets there makes things a little difficult for you in the reproductive area. So, you went through the whole adoption thing to make yourself feel more masculine and that is who you are on the golf course with now" said Karlotta smugly.

"Then what do you need my help for if you seem to know everything?" asked Hal angrily.

"I need you to investigate Trinity Health Insurance Company," said Karlotta

"What for?" asked Hal.

"It seems as though they are creating approval letters and not only is Trinity paying for the services which are not our concern. They have the members listed as having Caid-Care billed as a secondary insurer so we have been paying on services that should have been denied," said Karlotta.

"How do you know that these services should have been denied?" asked Hal.

"Many of them have no authorization number and this is probably because they could not generate one manually, I know that the legitimate letters have an authorization and it seems as though we have been picking up the tab for many of the approvals if Trinity Insurance did cover the service," said Karlotta.

"Ok, I'm on it. But you have to provide me with all of the claims that you can find that have this issue. I just want the ones that have us as secondary billing because it seems to me that the crooks at Trinity approved the letter and then had Trinity pay out and those approved claim payments were sent to another payment address and the money is then given to those involved in the scheme and as for Caid-Care's involvement when service was not covered by Trinity it was sent to Caid-Care and they are most likely working with other crooks inside the company who approve the services as a secondary payer to collect money on this scheme but they should know that when covered under managed care Caid-Care is not secondary insurance. They can use Caid-Care if the service is not covered but they cannot double bill Trinity by charging Caid-Care for the same service. This is what I think they are doing the facilities, hospitals, or even providers are being paid twice on a fraudulent approval letter. I'm taking this to mean that Trinity created itself as the socialized health insurance company for those who were not old enough to retire and for those who were too young to work or were unemployed or under-employed. The issue is the same, you have people who cannot afford to pay premiums to insurance companies of all ages due to underpaid conditions. The insurance companies have now appealed to the state for money to continue to provide services to their members because if the burden of this falls on Caid-Care it will overload the system in that if you think we are in a back log of auditing clams now, see what happens if companies like Trinity insurance goes out of business." said Hal.

"That won't affect the daily care of members because they can still see their doctor, but it may delay a visit if a claim is not processed or unpaid because Caid-Care gets backed up and claims take longer to process. This would complicate the system tremendously," said Karlotta.

"This investigation is going to take time because we have to identify the fraudsters behind the letters so we need a contact at Trinity Health Insurance Company so that we can find out how they are operating and what money each person has made so far. I'm sure for many of them it is as if they have a second job as they fraudulently create approval letters and are getting paid from the companies that benefit from having their services approved," said Hal.

"But Trinity was nicknamed the socialized health insurance for the rest of us and given that scenario, the commercial insurers are going to become a thing of the past since they are practically unaffordable. But what I don't understand is how can a system survive with healthcare costs rising and not many people being able to pay for health insurance premiums?" said Karlotta.

"Caid-Care will have problems if this continues, and Trinity will for the most part will go out of business. if they don't centralize into one company and allow each state that they operate to run their insurance. Everything hinges on the cost of living and provisions within each state. This will prevent the oversaturation of members getting care in one state as opposed to another. If New York is a preferred market for health care, then you will have someone from Florida saying, I have Trinity in Florida, so I stay with a relative in New York so that I can get the care that I need as opposed to receiving sub-standard care in the state they reside in." said Hal. "People need to put things in perspective. We need separate but equal types of care in this country so that no matter what economic status you are you get just about as good of the same healthcare as a person who is financially stable."

"Well, that's what I wanted to discuss with you now and I have to get busy in getting this information to you because it seems as though it is from several years' worth of doing, and if this is fraudulent we will never recoup this money that we paid out, so we will have to write it off as a loss, but we may be penalized for not noticing this earlier. But we were swamped with working so many claims honestly these things just were not noticed," said Karlotta.

"This won't go on for too long because a computerized system is coming and errors such as this will be weeded out and caught as soon as the claim is processed as opposed to auditing work and noticing it several years later," said Hal. "Now who is this contact person at Trinity so I can get started on this I have to make sure he is not involved in any way because if he is my contacting him will alert a cover-up. I will have to do a background check."

"His name is Tang Bor. He oversees internal audit at Trinity," said Karlotta.

"I will give him a call. Now you get your bottom-heavy ass back to work!" said Hal rudely as he hung up the phone and smiled at his adopted daughter.

Chapter Seventeen

"The special education teachers are complaining. This is way too much work for them," said Valdena Plantation as she sat on her sofa.

"This is exactly the reason we have to begin just to pass those who have learning issues through. We will call it social promotion so that they can get out into the world, and we will have people like Bren Chopper and Teneil Roner masquerade for them," said Mr. Deivers proudly.

"You know I just love it when we involve the aspect of 'mother' it makes it as if we don't have to do much as educators in the system. There are those who I don't want to teach because they will become able to do for themselves in life and not so much for others and we will then lose control of what we were always trying to establish even in these modern times." said Valdena Plantation whose husband had not yet come home from work.

"But what if they refuse?" asked Mr. Deivers. "That Teneil seems like a feisty one and I'm not too sure about her. She's smart and helpful to people but she does not have that integration characteristic that we need her to have."

"I know. She quite stubborn and I think we are going to have to work her over somewhat," said Valdena Plantation as she laughed.

Mr. Deivers became nervous. "Look no rough stuff. I know how sensitive you are about those who don't look like you, but you have inherited your great-grandfather's ways. I mean you got Teneil's class doing a lot of homework to compensate for what Quezel did not do and if they don't do the work then you whip out your big stick and beat them into submission. You know the parents are out either working several jobs to make ends meet or on the public assistance program and having to struggle though the system. Life was not easy for these people as the demands that were made on them continued. He wondered if people thought that oppression was sometimes worse than slavery. In slavery, there was no hope or very little of it and that was painful, but then there existed a pain of false hope in that you get there, and you see what you worked for all come apart and that in itself gives you no hope for the future. He knew oppression was just modern slavery because the outcome was the same.

"We have to condition them," said Valdena Plantation abruptly.

"We got these people going through all kinds of struggles and what not and you're saying they are not conditioned?" asked Mr. Deivers.

"They just got here.' said Valdena Plantation smugly.

"Oh, now I remember we brought the parents here and put them in the situations that we did. We didn't educate their parents and had them have families at a young age and then we began to remove the skills by modernization and denied them the work by not giving them or allowing them to continue the work in modernization. We displaced them in the process and then put them into the social service system to force them to do work that we wanted them to do without too much of an education and then when the money is not enough, we get them into the dark social survival such as drugs, prostitution, and crime." said Mr. Deivers as he was just testing Valdena Plantation.

"I said we must condition the children to do the work," said Valdena Plantation. "We cannot make our school system a resource for success for these people because if we were to do that what kind of system would we have?" she asked.

"You mean we don't want one of equality? So, if we educate these people we put them on the same level and we will no longer have them do the grunt or more tedious tasks. You know in commercials America is often portrayed as this beautiful pace that is war free and a place that one can call home. Pictures show a tranquil world that everyone loves, respects, and understands. We accomplished this by watering down history and sweeping it under the rug by hailing the civil rights leaders and pacifying the struggles of the people without ever solving or coming to an agreement about the issue." said Mr. Deivers.

"We must sell propaganda. If we don't do that how to we tout ourselves and do international business with other countries?" asked Valdena Plantation. "If we revealed we brought the foreigners here to displace those of afro-centric existence what would that say about the propaganda that we display in our commercials as though life is so easy and simple?" asked Valdena Plantation. We would be called hypocrites and liars and would not be one of the leaders of countries in this world. When we lure people to this land, we often take them and put them where we would like them to be. They have a purpose not denied by themselves but by what we want them to do with the opportunities that we allow for."

"We do not exactly use our caste system as propaganda to show for. It would be a turnoff for every foreigner to see that we have as much tolerance as South African. We can't let this be, so we have to make this integration of people as seamless as possible." said Mr. Deivers.

"I feel as though this is a burden because we have to condition the children to do the work and that often means mistreatment of them so that they will toughen up and be able to stand up to the pressures and duress we are about to put them under. I have to put energy into hate although it comes so easy," said Valdena Plantation as she got up and looked out of her living room window.

"It would be more of a burden to teach and put upon the intellect of those you would rather be under you. Many of our educators see resistance in teaching. It is seen as a conflict because you are educating those for professionalism and to have them enter the same economic level as one would. This was discussed in one of our off-color off-grid meetings if you know what I mean." said Mr. Deivers.

"You had a teacher's meeting that I wasn't invited to!" snapped Valdena Plantation.

"Now come deary don't get that big keister of yours in a bunch. You know you can't go to these things. I mean we tell you whats going on enough as it is but you can't be there. Sweetie, you know the family got rules and you got that bit of blood in you that we just cannot allow. Yes, it's across the board how we don't want to teach because we fear that we'd be losing control. So we take the education out of schools for those who can't do the work and condition those who can by passing the burden onto them. In doing so we prepared them to be twice as good and to them of course serve as being oppressed by those they will eventually have to work with in life. In creating this system, we now have a way to not teach who we don't want to teach and use them for those we socially promoted, we give the others or the preferred well-paying jobs and have those who are oppressed do much of the work." said Mr. Deivers mysteriously.

"My conditioning is my tough love towards these people. I don't want any write-ups or bad reports from you or any of my superiors. I expect for you to justify what I do even if an angry or irate parent comes into the school wondering why I beat their child or gave them too much work to do." said Valdena Plantation. " Now I must go because my husband will be here any moment."

"I know you like the upper hand." as for your choice in men!" said Mr. Deivers as he hung up the phone.

Teneil wiped her tears as she cried, and Bren watched her helplessly. "This is just way too much work for me to handle," she said. "The thing about it is that I never see Quezel doing any and she's older than I am."

"It's by design. We're compensating for what your sister and my brother do not do," said Bren. "It's sad but we are being used as the backbone so they can get ahead."

"If the school system is doing this or allowing this to be done. Then what's going to happen once we get into the working world?" said Teneil. "I love music and watching old movies it is like my father takes all the fun out of life. if it isn't one chore then I have to look after another. Lon Jr. is as they say intellectually disabled or mentally handicapped. My father won't even play ball with him or do father-son things with him. Who knows, maybe if it did it would help him." said Teneil as she struggled to compose herself.

"I'm having the same issues with my mother she won't have my sister help her in the kitchen, but she expects me to help her prepare the gourmet meals she so likes to eat. I mean if she spent time with her she could bond over skill and not have these upsets for attention. But my mom ain't hearing none of that." said Bren as he sympathized with Teneil.

"My father can whip some ass and he probably calls it quality time with the family when he does. But yet he says he has to earn a living to keep a roof over our heads so on the weekend unless he handing out whippings he doesn't want to hear about kids or spending time with them, especially mentally handicapped ones." said Teneil. "Bren, we're in high school and it seems like our childhood was one of struggle or..."

"Conditioning!" said Bren with a smile.

"Exactly, as if we are being so challenged and as you say conditioned so that we can be prepared for the lives we are going to be living. But I feel as though our parents have something to do with this because certain people are allowed to get away with things and we are not as if I am a field worker with a governing house negro." said Teneil.

"I don't think they want us to succeed. I mean even if we do it will be for a short time only because they need the sacrifice and us to play the role of the oppressed. That is the deal they made with the white man to keep their positions. Their treatment or conditioning of us is how they and the others escape the harsh treatment and how a system is created to ensure that people are not all equal." said Bren.

"I don't see any evil doing happening except to us and people like us, so this confirms what I have been thinking all along. My dad's strange behavior. I think they are informants, and we are being kept a certain way to be used for the good of superiority. I can't think of any other reason why things would be this difficult when life does not have to be that way." said Teneil.

"How can we prove or even accuse them of doing such a thing?" asked Bren who realized it was getting late and that his mother would be home from work and would ask him why his homework was not done and why he wasn't being more helpful to his sister."

"Give me a few days, but I'm going to figure this all out. My dad is known to people, and I know that he is an informant in some kind of way too. I just have to prove it." said Teneil.

"But even if you do prove it, how are you going to get the power to stop it?" asked Bren.

Chapter Eighteen

"Teneil you have got to study harder and get grades that are acceptable to get into college!" yelled Lon Roner.

Teneil cried, "I, I tried. I have a lot of homework and tests there are a lot of questions and some writing for so many subjects."

"Turn off that radio and concentrate. All you want to do is listen to your music and tune everybody else out," yelled Lon as if he were in the service.

"I do my chores and help around the house. Ok, I will stay up later to study more," she said as she hoped that this would be enough for him to shut the fuck up and leave her alone.

"Don't your schoolmates have homework?" asked Lon angrily. "I always see you talking to them or playing around but none of you ever seem serious about a damn thing. All you do is talk and laugh more than any person I have ever met." snapped Lon.

Teneil listened to her father as she began to think to herself as she wiped her tears. "Gosh, he seems to know all of this but he can never fix anything around the house and all he does is find fault in others to take the focus from himself. Teneil would notice that Quezel was only scolded a few times during their childhood. But when it came to her he would double or even triple the pain with his beating or yelling over things that he should be encouraging about. She knew that as a father there were kind moments that after a while turned to emancipation because she was so repulsed by him. Teneil was exhausted but she had a long way to go and she had to find a way to get through high school and even college. The put-downs or insults were that teachers told Lon that Teneil would never get that far. But she was puzzled because if she was in the humanities program then why would you treat her as a special education student? She once had a black teacher who wanted her to go to special education and she refused and then she had a white teacher who told her father that she would never make it through college.

Teneil worked hard despite the time that she found to be a kid for just a little while. Being a kid wasn't acceptable to Lon Roner. He needed Teneil to grow up and be an adult in a hurry. Teneil always went to school and did everything with home in mind. It was all becoming too much. The fact that Quezel was the older sister did not help and the teachers never said anything insulting about her. Teneil could not go to her for advice about regents testing or even SATs, because she never saw Quezel take any. Teneil knew she had to rely on herself. Her father Lon would only brag over and over about his accomplishments as if he had no help in the world. But Teneil knew that Lon knew how to get over. He was a southerner who was rooted in using the epistle on people as a way to defend himself from the transgressions of the time he had done. If you could take someone and make them sacrifice for things over and over then you have a sacrificial lamb for offering that anyone would accept and she knew he would use her to get by with all of the things he didn't want to do or things that he knew he shouldn't be doing but would use her to sacrifice for. Lon never demanded that his children go to church, and she knew that he took all of his days while living in the South and came up north to make it a testimony of sorts.

Jacel looked at Teneil and waited for Lon to calm down. "Please, let Teneil do her homework now. You've upset her and she's going to think that we are the most horrible people in the world"

"Teneil, go to your room and do your homework," Jacel said as if she were saying something of invention. That was what Teneil started to do until Lon saw her report card and he decided that it was not good enough. Which was strange because she never heard him say anything about Quezel's report card or grades.

Teneil did as her mother told her and went to her room she began to cry again. "I can't do much more than I am already doing. She began to focus on all of the assignments that she had and realized that in an independent study class she did some of her homework already. She looked up and Quezel had entered their bedroom.

"Let me guess dinner is later because you had an argument with dad about your report card," said Quezel.

"How did you know?" asked Teneil.

"As soon as I came in dad happily greeted me and then as he drank his orange soda, he told me about your grades which I thought weren't bad but I was a little surprised because I felt you could improve on some of the subjects that you have. There is afterschool help and tutoring to help you. I know you like your sports, but your grades are more important because he's expecting you to go to college and you won't be able to get into a four-year institution with your grades as others get higher grades and you will put mom and dad to shame. said Quezel. "You have to be able to compete."

"I think that is the least of their worries because there is always community college and from then, I can go to a four-year college. People have gone on and graduated from college with grades worse than mine. I know I will get in somewhere." said Teneil as she continued to finish up her homework.

Teneil knew that her parents had given Quezel the pep talk about her and had her go upstairs and lecture her since she is the older sister. But she felt that Quezel should practice what she preaches. Quezel lectured her and her parents made a big stink about it so that they would take the focus off of Quezel not doing any work. This way parents and teachers would only concentrate on Teneil and want to punish her for everything. Teneil knew that teachers like Valdena Plantation were behind this, and she had to find a way to get from under the torture. But Teneil knew that as long as she was in the school system, they had plans for her. The conditioning to prepare her for what was to come of her life often scared her.

"Aren't you going to do your homework?" asked Teneil.

Quezel became defensive knowing she didn't do very much. "I already did it." she quickly said.

"When?"

"I was over Wendor's house, and I ate dinner there also and now I'm going back out," said Quezel.

"Over to Wendor's?" asked Teneil.

"Uh, no I have other plans," said Quezel.

"So did Wendor and her family." giggled Teneil

"What do you mean by that?" asked Quezel.

"Oh, nothing. I just noticed that they seem so some-timey," said Teneil.

"Look just concentrate on your homework and what not and stop worrying about what I am doing. This is all about you and what you have to get done and accomplish in life. Mommy and Daddy are expecting a lot of you, and you should not let them down." said Quezel.

"Why don't they expect the same of you?" asked Teneil.

"You're the smart one, so more is asked of you," said Quezel.

"I don't understand why you can't do your contribution. Why does it always have to be me, me, me?" asked Teneil angrily.

"Why not you? I said you are the smarter one," said Quezel as she got up to leave the room as their mother Jacel entered.

"Teneil I have been calling you for several minutes. Why didn't you answer me?" asked Jacel.

"I didn't hear you," said Teneil in defense of herself.

"She was busy asking me multiple choice questions and didn't hear you that's why. I told her to go eat because dad was eating but she was too afraid to go downstairs after he chewed her out so she didn't want to go. I told her she had to be able to handle things and if she can't handle an argument or two in the home what good will she be in life?" asked Quezel.

"You said no such thing, stop lying!" yelled Teneil.

"Listen you have to get it together and stop taking your poor grades out on everyone. It is not productive," said Quezel.

"And when you're finished eating Teneil the dishes have to be done," said Jacel.

"Dishes!" snapped Teneil.

"Yes, it's your turn tonight," said Jacel.

"Nope, I did them last night and the night before because Quezel came home really late," said Teneil. "How could you forget this?" asked Teneil. "So, it's Quezel's turn."

"I can't do them tonight because I have somewhere to go and I will be back late and dad does not like the kitchen left dirty," said Quezel.

"Well, you best get back here before then so you can get them done." snapped Teneil.

"You don't tell me what to do. I'm the one who tells you what to do. Now, stop feeling sorry for yourself, get your homework done and stop daydreaming off into the world of music and do the dishes as your mother asked you to. You're making things difficult for everyone around here." said Quezel. "I'll be back later, dad's giving me a ride."

"Where's dragon mouth going?" asked Teneil.

"He has a meeting with Mr. Deivers." said Jacel.

"All I know is that it gets late to have meetings of this sort out in the boonies. Why can't he just talk by phone?" asked Teneil.

"Because the meetings are about mentally handicapped people and there are several people in attendance, now come eat and do the dishes and if it's not too late you can watch TV before you get ready for bed," said Jacel.

Lon Roner drove down a deserted street and entered the Cleary Building. He grabbed a soda and a few snacks and sat down at a long table with several other people. He spotted a woman whom he recognized and thought he saw her as he left work the other day. The meeting went on and on for a few hours as people took notes and offered suggestions. Finally, it was time to go. People exited the Cleary Building and the woman waited as she knew Lon would approach her.

"Can I give you a ride to your car?" he asked.

"Sure." said the woman.

"You still got that ass on you like you was a Black woman who was dipped in bleach." laughed Lon.

The woman reached over and kissed Lon as she got into the car. "I missed you she said."

"When did you get back in town?" he asked.

"I have been here for a while. It's just of a enough distance to be close to you and enough distance to be away from your wife." said the woman.

"You were leaving AUXY the other day, weren't you?" asked Lon.

"Yes, rumor has it that they may be merging with Blue Onx another computer business. Should I take the job or do you have one to offer me?" asked the woman named Elkin Khann.

Lon kissed Elkin and wondered if she was going to be a warehouse worker to make ends meet and what was she doing in the Cleary Building.

Chapter Nineteen

Hal Keskar fumbled to speak when he tried to call Tang. "Uh hello," he said. "May I speak with Ku Tang or Tang Ku?"

Tang became angry. "Ku Tang is my ex-wife. I am in the middle of a messy divorce because she lay with many, many men. She also plotted to kill me." said Tang regretfully.

"Oh, I am sorry to hear that. But if she plotted to kill you why isn't she in jail?" asked Hal Keskar.

"She has connections and tried to make killing me look like an accident. She said it was my fault because I ate the food that she had as an experiment. I had awful food poisoning that I'm still trying to get over, now what can I do for you?' he asked.

'There seems to be an issue with claims that are being billed to Caid-Care from Trinity Health Insurance it seems that we are getting a lot of claims as the secondary payer when Trinity should be paying the entire claim.

"Many members who have Trinity Health Insurance also have Caid-Care. Caid-Care pays for things that Trinity Health Insurance does not cover," said Tang who did not want to go through every claim.

"But that is the point, many of these approvals that were issued through Trinity should have also been paid by you guys and we are receiving claims that are kicked back to you because Trinity is saying they don't cover certain services," said Mr. Keskar.

"You have to understand that with each approval letter there is no guarantee of payment so with that being said if you look into the contracts for certain services Caid-Care should automatically kick in because Trinity only allows for a certain number of services according to the medical need of the member. said Tang who was drinking a tonic to help ease the pain.

"The problem is that we did a preliminary investigation and we found that there were approval letters that were supposed to have been approved by a doctor and the doctor has no record of doing the approval in their Trinity database. This is concerning because if the approval was not reviewed by a nurse and then approved by a doctor then who initiated the approval and why is that not reflected somewhere in the member's chart?" asked Mr. Keskar who seemed aggravated.

Tang was seemingly disinterested in what Mr. Keskar was saying. He could not believe that he had fallen for a woman who just wanted to use him for the programs that he designed in his spare time and the money he generated while she was sleeping around with other men. She lied to him about being a scientist at a hospital and was a paid killer for a group of people who did intelligence search control and if they felt threatened by an individual, they would make plans to eliminate them. Tang was hurt and distraught over the fact that his marriage was over and that he had nothing to show for it. It did not matter to him that he had a well-paying job at Trinity and other things in the works to make a name for himself. He wanted love in the human aspect of love. He filled his time with work and other interests. Loving his ex-wife proved to be damaging. She wanted half of all his assets and was upset about who she gave them to. Tang knew this was how his ex-wife did business. This plagued and bothered Tang and he presented this to his attorney in hopes to settle out of court. He knew his wife was still trying to kill him as she wanted to take hold of his intellectual collection and sell them to the highest bidder and then kill him so that he would never reap the benefits.

"This is the first I am hearing of this." admitted Tang. "I will have to get my team working on retrieving all of the approval letters in question. But tell me, do you have any letters we can research now?" he asked.

"Several have come in to raise concern because if these members are seeing private doctors and not doctors who are enrolled or appointed by the state Caid-Care will not pay because they are not participating.

This means the provider is out-of-network and you are putting the member in the situation of having to pay for services that are not affordable to them," said Mr. Keskar as he noticed that many of the charges added up to quite a large bill that was not affordable to most people on Caid-Care.

"This argument can be presented as a hearing to the State or an appeal to the insurance company, but I need the authorization numbers to have my team look into what physician or nurse reviewed the approval and for what service. Without that information to go on we will not be able to do much about payments either recouped or otherwise," said Tang.

"I will work on getting those to you but in the meantime, you need to get a rooster of all the work approved and reviewed by the doctors at Trinity this way it will make it easier to search through. I'm sorry to hear that you are going through all of this and I hope that this all gets resolved in your favor," said Mr. Keskar. "Several years ago I cheated on my first wife something awful. We were both young and I enjoyed spanking the monkey with her so to speak. After a while, it became boring as I saw so much beauty at work and I went for it. My ex-wife tried to kill me several times. It got to the point that I had to sleep with the lights on and I had to eat before I came home and after I left for work because anything she fed me made me ill. One day I politely told her that instead of making each other miserable that we should just part ways because we had kids together and we had to focus on that part of our lives and not make things about us anymore. She finally agreed after exposing me to my former employer who fired me for having dalliances with his wife. Strangely enough, she divorced him and we have been happily married ever since." said Mr. Keskar.

"Now what about your ex?" asked Tang.

"Well, she married my former boss and now I'm pushing paper and she helped him grow his company into a Fortune 500 company and they have expanded and done very well. My kids are in good schools as a result and the sweet thing about it is that I got away without having to pay any child support. Now, each of us had more children by our new partners but my kids by my ex don't call me as much because my ex and her husband are so loaded that they don't rely on me and they pretty much get anything they want. My wife has to work as do I so we can make ends meet. I don't know if my new wife regrets the decisions she made when we were having a fun time. But her life has changed a lot. I can't afford all of the things she had in her first marriage. She rarely complains or mentions that she wishes she had more in life or compares me to her ex-husband. I think when he was focused on building his company, he neglected her and she hated him for that." said Mr. Keskar. "My first wife was and still is such a dig, she looks for money and when she couldn't pull it by squeezing my cheeks, she became cruel to me and I sought happiness elsewhere, But I'm glad it ended the way it did because we both got what we wanted and it made it good for the kids also."

Tang thought and found where his wife was hanging out and decided to give these places a try as he became confident again in searching for love. "There has to be someone out there for him," he mumbled to himself. "Ok. Mr. Keskar, I will be talking to you." said Tang as he hung up the phone and realized that many of these claims would have to go through a hearing process to get paid if the money was ever recouped by Trinity.

Tang looked through his Rolodex to find Benita Drendel's number. He knew that she did letters for the company, but what he didn't know was that the Klan had a religious part in running Trinity Insurance Company in that if the money was recouped by the insurance company and it was found during a hearing that services were not approved then a member would be responsible for payment and a facility could deny services to the member if they did not receive payment. Benita knew this and would always make people unlike herself responsible for paying out-of-pocket. The process of computerizing older authorization numbers was underway, and Tang ran a queue of claims to see if any of the claims that were done matched up with the doctors and nurses who reviewed them and had them approved. That was when Tang realized that Benita was involved in a scheme in which she was not only making money for herself but making sure that minorities paid money out of pocket if the service was not paid for by the insurance company. Tang had to tell someone and he had to do so soon. Trinity was now in the red because of all of the money they had paid out and being overloaded with members who were sick and hospitalized. Trinity had to put some of the costs off on Caid-Care to avoid being flagged by the State as insolvent. Caid-Care would surely report them if they began to suspect a scam or fraud of sorts and then things would all go crashing down because he realized that Benita, Stace and their cult of people had found a way to supplement their income and make poor people pay as a result. He had to go through all of the letters that Benita, Stace along with their associates did to get something on her before he could report her to compliance and have the bogus approvals investigated. This was going to take some work but he had to get started soon because the poorer members of Trinity will soon be billed by their providers or facilities by being out-of-network with Caid-Care if not paid for by Trinity. But why would Benita and Stace do this? The answer was plain and simple. They hated working for a company that employed minorities in various positions and they used this to make money by mocking Trinity for employing minorities. They knew if they did this Trinity would go out of business and this would affect poor and minority people that they cared nothing about, and she could take her trash can ass onto a commercial insurance company.

Chapter Twenty

Life was not any easier for Teneil as she had finally entered college. Teneil hated the fact that she was never able to make her own decisions about things which was the actual dilemma in her life. She hated being away at college and knew that her father did this to divide and conquer things. If she were to go away, then she would be of no help to Quezel who worked sporadically and she could have at least been of assistance to her so that if they were in the same college or even a community one Quezel would get an associate's degree and she would not have to depend on Teneil for school cred once they entered the workforce. Lon Roner was an angry man who always wanted something for himself. There was nothing wrong with that, but he had not learned how to think his way across the street or to walk through an open door. For a man to claim he did not need anybody to give him anything, if you just open the door, he will get it himself, he sure depended on people to not only open the door but to get things for him. This was evident because he sent her away to a college that was unlike her high school. and this experience was something to be desired. Sure, there were people like her, but she was bothered by the fact that the place was so spread out. It was like being on a never-ending plantation that had acres and acres of land with no end. Teneil knew she did not have the kind of curiosity to explore the island and vowed to return home to be closer to the city and not hoarded up on some plantation as if this were some kind of funny farm joke. Teneil liked the city life and as a loner, she could find her way by roaming in and out of all the culture and diversity the city had to offer. Lon, her father would never accept this. For Teneil to be the religious vessel he wanted her to be he sent her to places that reminded him of the South where she would learn a way of life despite the schools only being integrated on the surface. She did not question why because she knew the answer to modern-day slavery. Lon was an informant who for the most part used Quezel to find his next physical attraction and then used Teneil to get it. Things had gone sour with Elkin as Lon saw her for many a year but as she got older Lon was less attracted to her and was looking for a younger version. It seemed as though he found it as that was how Lon decided what college Teneil was going to. As an informant to the KKK Lon would find out the inner talks with people in certain circles and report information back to Kib who then, in turn, evaluated it with his other superiors if people were deemed a threat, then Lon would help eliminate or separate people. The black population had grown significantly, and Lon knew this would be a concern. He liked to see people who looked like him who were down and out and who asked him for spare change. Lon was assuredly the house negro and wanted to remain that way.

"She does not like being there." snapped Jacel.

"She's got to learn independence and how to do things for herself," yelled Lon as they sat in their living room.

"She can learn independence by just doing what she has always been doing. She suggested going to a college nearby or even in the city but for some reason, you wouldn't allow it and I find it strange. All the money we are spending."

"She needs to get a good education and that's why I sent her here where I did," said Lon.

"She could have also got a good education by going to one of the city colleges and helping Quezel."

"Quezel does not need her help and she is doing everything she is supposed to be doing. I want this to stop about you wanting the two of them to do college together as if they are still in high school," said Lon angrily.

"I just think that there is another way to go about things and constantly isolating Teneil from people is not going to do any good," said Jacel she needs city interaction.

"Look, you whiney idiot! There are people on that campus the dorms are full, most people room together and they have all kinds of activities to keep her busy. I don't think she needs the city as much as you think, and she should learn to interact with everyone and not just her own." said Lon who became very hostile towards Jacel.

"Don't call me names like that because you seem to be the one who is doing all of the whining. Now, I know you're getting ready to go out to another one of your meetings again so why don't you get to it," said Jacel in defense of herself.

"Look, I work as a consultant and I have to maintain a certain client base to keep money coming in," said Lon.

"It was cheaper for the company to outsource and hire you the way they did so that they are not responsible for your health insurance and other perks that a company may provide. But in the long run, they are not saving any money because it may be cheaper to hire you because of all the hot air you give them and the time they pay you to complete a task. Now, I may not know much but you are doing more work for yourself which is unnecessary especially when you can find a job elsewhere making about the same amount of money." said Jacel as she got up to do the dishes.

"I'm my own boss and I do as I please and that's the difference!" said Lon as he watched Jacel leave the living room for the kitchen.

Lon got into his car and drove to another part of town where there were large houses and several park benches. He got out of the car and sat on a bench and pretended to read the paper and the Kib pulled up and parked his car and motioned for Lon to get in. Lon walked over and got into the car.

"Don't tell me, she wants Teneil to get out of that fancy university and go someplace cheaper because she wants a new car to match the kitchen you did for her." laughed Kib.

"It was sort of a bribe. If she ever found out that I was making Teneil the field negro by sending her to that spread-out plantation of an up-and-coming university she would never forgive me. And not that it matters because I am not looking for her forgiveness. She just needs to understand that in this world where they are only going to allow a certain number of people through and for me to make my money somebody is going to have to sacrifice." said Lon.

"Now, you have to understand population control. Some of those field negros are smart and they become a threat to the have children and have the opportunity and the mindset to educate themselves and do wonderful things. She can't have any children because her intelligence is a threat to our superiority. We were lucky enough to get you to play along with us. You're doing well for a guy whose roots are from the South. Now, I know you can't be a part of us but we need you to continue our mission." said Kib.

"Once Teneil gets out of school, we have to put her in the environment that will enable her to do all of what we had planned and that includes being sent back to the fields because people with learning handicaps do not thrive well in busy academia. We have arranged that once your kind has kids if they have more than one or even two of them, we make them leave the workforce and go through the system. This enables us to give jobs to our kind and have others in subservient positions. Even if they have kids and have a job, they get paid through the system to keep a roof over their head and food in the bellies of their children." said Kib proudly.

"So, if I take Teneil and use or barter her for the transgressions of Jacel's family and issues with Quezel and my shit that I got going on..." said Lon.

"Yes, you can remain the house negro and you do not have to worry about it. What we want is to be able to take our children who would normally be put on disability due to them not being able to work doing advanced technical stuff and put them in an office and just let them stay there during the day and have people like Teneil do the work," said Kib.

"But don't you think that an office full of busy people will notice that you have someone with a learning disability collecting a huge paycheck while doing nothing and you have all of the other workers doing a lot more for less? Won't somebody complain?" asked Lon.

"That is why we have her in that isolated area of the soon-to-be university. She will work on the outskirts of town in a rather isolated area. This is where we will put our people with mental or learning issues so that they appear normal and have progressed through school." said Kib. "If we put them in a busy environment and start giving them assignments to do. It will be just like being in school again and you know that we doubled up on the pressure on Teneil so that we don't suffer the religious repercussions of having to socially promote Wendor, Marlie, Quezel, and others that are like them. Of course, someone will notice and then the work will suffer, and the company will go out of business. This is why we need people like Teneil to do a day thing work program in a smaller setting so that they don't put companies out of business by hiring people who cannot do the work." said Kib as he thought he heard something.

"Look I understand all of this, but this seems like it's going to take a long time," said Lon.

"The plan is to waste as much time out of the lives of people like Teneil. What we do is to increase the master race and we will have Wendor, Quezel, and Marlie have children and even get married so that we don't have a planet that we are all afraid of and once that happens they get to enter the workforce because they will be people like Teneil to do all of the work so that they don't have to worry about not being intelligent enough to do it," said Kib.

"That will work for me and she's going to understand that this has to work for her also. Now I have to get going. It's getting late and now you see why I love the city so much, it's dark over here." laughed Lon. "I suppose Teneil is going to have to get by the best way she can once she goes to work in the boonies. And I vowed to Elkin that I would help Drecker because she reminds me so much of Quezel."

"Ok, I suppose I'll see you around. You did well by offering to become a consultant after that last merger. I'll talk to you later." said Kib as he watched Lon get out of his car and they both drove off.

Big Troy and Bren Chopper were hiding behind a bush where they heard the entire conversation. "See man, they meet up here where I told you and discuss their plans for the world," said Big Troy.

"Now all I have to do is tell Teneil." said Bren.

"That would be too messy, we have to find another way to help her," said Big Troy.

"Come on," said Bren. "We got to be on our way to the night shift at the bank."

Chapter Twenty-One

"Look I know you don't think much of him but he's, my husband!" yelled Jacel Roner into the phone.

"There is a rumor going around saying that Lon is an informant." Jacel laughed. "Informant, you mean he hooked up with the feds?" she asked.

"No." said the woman.

"You mean he didn't come from the South like he told me and he from another country?" asked Jacel.

"Not exactly." the woman.

"Then what?" asked Jacel.

"He in on it with the Klan." said the woman who was laughing on the other end.

"The Klan!" yelled Jacel.

"No that cannot be. Lon hates white people because of the way he was treated in the South. He constantly tells me and the kid's stories about having to go to the back of a lunch counter to try and get food and sitting at the back of the bus. I have no idea what you are talking about and why you are trying to start rumors about a man as good as Lon. He gets up and goes out to work every day and I don't starve and got a roof over my head." said Jacel in defense of Lon.

"Girl, he not all that. The man you married was like a high school equivalent diploma. Sure, you got a roof over your head but you got your minion Teneil running around the house doing all kinds of chores and being invisible as a child. This helps him out because you know if he had to do his part of any sacrifice, he would be bent over on somebody's lap." laughed the woman.

Jacel became angry. She and Latrina had been friends for many, many years and Latrina calls her to berate Lon. "Something else must be happening to cause this." Jacel said to herself.

"Listen, I usually have Teneil home on some weekends to help me out around the house and I will ask her if she sees a Klan robe or something hidden around here," said Jacel as she laughed.

"What's wrong with you doing a little looking around yourself? Lon gon get mad at you or something?" asked Latrina. "It's like when he is at work, he's the nicest thing you come in contact with but when he is home he is just an awful being. Cursing y'all out and getting hand happy to the point where you need the police to intervene or walk around traumatized looking. Sometimes people think y'all shell shocked or something." giggled Latrina.

"So, you called here to laugh at my family and insult Lon?" asked Jacel.

"No girl, I'm trying to help you." she said honestly. "Rumor has it he buddy-like with a guy who is known to be a Klan member and that he got Lon seeing white women behind your back," said Latrina who shook her head pathetically.

"He's seeing other women?" asked Jacel. "He can't be. He calls me from work, or I call him and he usually returns my calls and although he works late he usually calls me and then if he does not take a cab I usually pick him up, and he doesn't be smelling like funk grit or like he came out from somebodies cocoon. So, I don't know where you getting all of this gossip but it doesn't sound like the Lon I know."

"Girl, you are still naive. This man has been playing you for years. Now he is not into color. He was one of those southerners who were displaced and felt abandoned by their states, so his attraction to white women reminds him of home and how he wished things could be different, so he always looks to bond with them and not so much his people." said Latrina.

"So now you a psychologist?" asked Jacel.

"Girl, I been through every part of this ghetto and got to know people from the other side. Now I love you and Lon and the kids too, but the damn girl the man is strange, and he craves for the comforts of home and acceptance. He was asked to spy for the man, and he saw that as an opportunity to be a part of their lives and regain what he did not have in the South while he was growing up." said Latrina as she tried to find a reason for Lon's ways.

"He just likes to be to himself, and the job does put demands on him and I think he tries to fit in," said Jacel.

"Honestly, the man does not like himself because of how he looks and wishes to be anything but. So, he sells out basically or as our history continues to evolve from its past he has become the house-negro of sorts at that company he works for," said Latrina.

"You mean Blue Onx?" asked Jacel.

"Whatever, I mean he told me the name the last time I saw y'all, but it just went out of my head. Now I know he makes good money, and he got out of college himself a few years ago, but believe me the house negro gets plenty advantage than the field negro and he dun made Teneil the field negro." I just don't think she deserves to have so deep a role because you being kind of harsh on the girl for no real reason except to spare the rod for your other children." said Latrina, "Now you know girl, we been through it and I'm not telling you how to raise em' because we going through this together but you really gon make her resentful because Teneil got ambition and want to do things with her life. She's a city girl believe it or not and not one to wander in the sticks and feel uncomfortable around people who don't look like her or appease their ignorance because they don't have her I want to achieve ways about herself. So he really going in the wrong direction."

Jacel thought to herself as she and Latrina considered each other family but it bothered her that she seems to be questioning or even doubting the way Lon and she were raising their children. None of the other people they grew up with had children that were so-called high achievers. Of course, there were a few people she met after she and Lon were married whose children went off to college and seemed to be doing very well but the majority of people had regular jobs and were no different from Teneil and Quezel.

"We think Teneil needs to be tougher because she is going to have more of a challenge," said Jacel.

"Why is it that he can't work with Lon Jr. to make him more manageable because as he gets older, he will be under the supervision of the State and he will have to be evaluated in doing so?" asked Latrina.

Jacel took a deep breath a few times and became tearful. "Because when I mention his son, he tears up, becomes emotional and does not want to talk about him, and refuses to do anything with him," said Jacel.

"What about yourself?" asked Latrina.

"The girls keep me busy, and I have other things to do around the house," said Jacel as she fumbled for excuses.

"Nope, you know you and Lon got this thing all worked out. Neither of you do not plan on doing shit. Now you need to get Quezel in a program where she can learn a skill so she doesn't go from job-to-job blood-draining Teneil into helping her because you will use her to barter and use the program that Lon Jr. is in to get favors for bartering Teneil into different low paying jobs so that both of your girls will look like the regular typical people you see. Now, I know that as a southerner Lon one of those has em' see through it. So, he ain't go do nothing but torturing Teneil into making Lon Jr. a more manageable person. This takes the responsibility from you because you feel it is too much and it evens out the fact that your husband does not want to spend time with his son. This also helps the special education teachers out. They can slack off of what they are doing with kids like Lon Jr. because they are not following the curriculum, they set out for family time with Lon to help with his progress. I know this is a lot on you Jacel but for Lon to want to use his southern roots on a girl who was bread in the North is unfair. All you have to do is take a swing with all the bases you got loaded and see how far she goes which means she gon end up living with you for several minutes and not have a life of her own. Jacel how can you do this?" asked Latrina.

"I thank you for your concern. But honestly, Teneil never complains about what she does around the house and is quite helpful and does not notice all that we give her to do. The college will teach her the intellect or enhance it and her father, and I won't have to worry about things in the future." said Jacel as she seemed confident that Teneil could do the job.

"Girl, I hope you realize all that you doing to this girl and that people don't look at you as some government extension by putting a roof over her head and giving her three meals day and clothes to wear. Although you instilled the work ethic in her while she was in her teens and that was good because she learned the value of money because Lon being comfortable with your scheming mother because when she asks y'all to sacrifice he knows he doesn't have to do anything to the house but let it fall apart into squalor, he can keep the car until it becomes a collector's item and he can wear his suit and tie or white boy dress downs to work as if he is taking care of things. Now on your side of town, things should be more spruced, I walk in, and I would think you are on section 8 the way you have things. Now Jacel we both grew up poor but to have Teneil live this way and not establish her independence and live the way she wants to be unfair. I just hope the girl doesn't become resentful of you. She's creative and should be allowed to do more but you shelter her and put her in the trashiest of situations to even things out with other family members instead of making them step up their game. If she were allowed to be that city girl instead of some barter and commodity from the sticks and I know that's what Lon gon do because that's where all the house negros send their children, then she would go further along." said Latrina as she gulped down some vodka.

"Teneil will learn to understand," said Jacel as if she were trying to convince herself but still didn't see where the concern was because Teneil always seemed so happy-go-lucky.

"But will she ever accept it?" asked Latrina.

"I'll worry about that when the time comes," said Jacel.

"The man doesn't like his people and he keeps it so that he stays the house negro and the others who should be as successful stay in the fields or got some kind of sacrifice to pay. I know he's an informant when I see one. Look, I gotta go. I still got to finish my cooking." said Latrina.

"For the man who loves white women. I have some leftovers heating up," said Jacel with a laugh. "I know how to compete."

Jacel hangs up the phone and decided not to worry about what Latrina was telling her because she always knew so much. Latrina turns to Lessy and says, "That man of hers is out of her hands and he needs to go to somebody who can handle him. Now speaking of men Lessy I got a lead on where Big Troy works."

"Girl, you dun answered my prayers!" said Lessy.

Chapter Twenty-Two

"Having Wendor learn a skill is not the answer!" yelled Kib as he stared at Benita.

"I'm sure she must have some kind of talent," assured Benita. Benita was making up their bed and she noticed that Kib would either sleep in another room or his armchair. Benita thought it was because of his back because he complained about it so much, but she realized that he had become quite distant and cold.

"Benita, I don't want any of my children being a hostess in a restaurant or fast food place because they are not able to do the school thing like their peers. We controlled the situation throughout all of their lives by manipulating the school system and it was to our advantage because the people in our communities were close-knit and we got to know each other over the years. I just don't think that having Wendor go away to school was the answer. We did her a disservice when we took her out of the community because there was no one to look after her in a sense due to her educational needs and she got in with some unsavory people." said Kib reluctantly as he took his time getting dressed for work.

"The school year is over and Wendor does not have to go back there if she does not want to. With that being said you should spend some time with her and get her into one of the local colleges and see if that is something she is interested in doing," said Kib.

"Why do I have to take her?" asked Benita. "You are the one who is always pushing this college thing on people. She can do other things that don't require a degree and I wish you would stop making it as though that all there is out there is a job that one needs a college degree for."

"Benita, things are changing, and I wish you would get with it instead of getting our children into low-paid careers just to have them rely on the system to get by. It's not fair to them and it's certainly not fair to us." said Kib. "Now, get your mind out of work for a moment and think about the girls because pretty soon we won't have much more control over their lives."

"You're forgetting religion, Kib" said Benita cheerfully. "I was talking to Mr. Deivers wife, and we seemed to have found a solution to our problems."

"Which is?" asked Kib.

"I'm our Klan meetings we discussed using those that are not of our purity to help us as if they were still enslaved all due in part to the thirteenth amendment that would allow those under such religious scrutiny to be used in that manner. So, I think we can at some point work out a deal by using people like Teneil Roner. It isn't all so bad Kib." said Benita who knew how to be resourceful. She managed to pay the bills for the family with the extra money she earned approving letters for various agencies while Kib spent his money on drinking, motels, and women.

"When can we start? and how can we be sure that Teneil won't rebel or not do what is asked of her," asked Kib.

"Lon is her father, right? asked Benita.

"Here is the thing Benita we have a different relationship with Lon than we do Teneil. With Lon, we always treated him as the house negro, the Uncle Tom and he been getting over like I don't know what. We do just enough to get by at Blue Onx because they want us to develop all kinds of sophisticated programs for applications and we don't have the patience or the know-how to do this sort of thing. So, we keep it simple and rehash older programs and get things to work for us. Blue Onx may not be pleased but it works, and Lon plays along so I'm not going to tell him all that we planned for people who are the field negros because he may think we are going too far or fear the repercussions if Teneil is not able to handle it. Although, I tell him what he needs to know, and he is in agreement." said Lon as looked at himself in the mirror.

"Jacel from what I understand has had Teneil trained from the get and she's quite a helper and we want her to be that way when she comes to work in these quiet little isolated towns that we try to keep the hellions out of. But I also hear that she can be a bit of a rebel but once we keep her busy enough, she won't have time to much of one." said Benita.

"I'm heading off to work now, and I got a few meetings lined up for today so if you don't hear from me that's what's going on," said Kib.

Benita had already taken the day off and was hoping Kib would decide to do the same. "Ok, I guess I will see you later." said quietly.

Kib left the house without kissing Benita. Kib lied about going to work. Work was the last thing he had on his mind. He drove over to the motel and Latrel was waiting for him but this time she was fully clothed.

Kib walked into the motel room and looked at Latrel and said, "Is that any way to treat a man who still finds you insanely attractive."

"We gotta talk, boy!" said Latrel in a serious manner.

"About?" asked Kib.

"About how my Lil running around with your ding-a-ling has eroded your family finances and your wife has been doing so illegal business on the side as a result," said Latrel.

"Illegal business?" asked Kib. "I'm afraid I don't understand."

Latrel shook her head. "You been getting lots of sugar with me for a moment now and you're carousing around, hanging out and spending a few dollars here and there it all adds up. What you give your wife to pay the bills with she may as well move back home with mama. But she was the type to save face and like all of the other schoolgirls she married or at least got a man and seemingly has a happy perfect family. Your wife works for Trinity and they got some high-priced insurance plans that turn me off no matter how much the government assists people. Anyways, I heard through a friend of mine that Benita has been doing a Lil crafty work on letters so that certain companies can get paid because the services are approved by the insurance company. The thing is with all this automation going on, they have been auditing Trinity and this uh, friend of mine is concerned that her Lil side money deal with Benita is going to go up in smoke. So, you may want to clean out that chimney of yours because it will keep you warmer and save you money by using the fireplace without her working or being in the slammer is going to put our relationship to the test. I figure heating costs you can do without because you could use the fireplace. You can also use it for cooking and washing the dishes by hand when you put water in a pail so that should save you on heat and water. As a hobby the kids can take up soap making and that will keep them clean, and you won't need to shop for things you can make yourself and this goes for clothes also. I know a wonderful seamstress who can teach your girls how to make a wardrobe for next to nothing. You need to refinance your house so that you can make lower monthly payments and use your backyard to grow food and get a freezer to store it in or jars to preserve things."

Kib looked at Latrel and smiled as he lit a cigarette. "What about entertainment?"

Latrel laughed. "I suppose board games will have to do. You will not have that allowance money to splurge on this motel because you will be talking public transportation to work and keeping the car for emergencies."

"You said she been doing some illegal letters, how'd you find out about this?" asked Kib.

"Like I said before my girl Pootie works for Trinity and she is in on the scheme because they got her from working from the government subsidies. It's one of the safety net deals that the government got going to prevent homelessness and hunger. Pootie got hired through the system and Trinity has a contract from the government to hire workers, and this is a tax advantage for them so that people like Pootie can work off her rent, food, utilities and other needs. This way Trinity does not have to pay people money to work, and they also don't have to give out benefits because these people are on the welfare system so they get their benefits from the system.

"If your friend Pootie got food, shelter, and clothes then what else does she want?" asked Kib.

"The system is always giving vouchers and checks so that very little cash changes hands. Although, there is a rumor going around that they will be using cards soon, so Pootie likes cash to do things with so doing them letters for Trinity allows her a chance to make money on the side," said Latrel.

"Now, their ends and scraps you been giving me is my cash, flow, and entertainment so if your wife ends up fired or in jail that is going to put a damper on things. Unless of course, you do as I suggested."

Kib thought to himself as he was not ready to give Latrel up. Benita held their family down but she could have as easily worked two jobs. He wondered about Benita at times because she was always taking the lazy way out of things. This included having Wendor learn a skill instead of finding a way for her to finish college. Kib could never approach Benita about this because she would want to know how he found out and would probably deny it. It wasn't for him to worry about if Benita would be fired or even jailed. That was her problem because she made the decision. Kib walked over and lay down on the bed and took a sip of whiskey from a bottle he had in his pocket.

"You look tired, Kib and it's not even noon yet," said Latrel.

"I got a lot on my mind, now come on over here and get comfy with me. Besides, I gotta find a way to move you in to help me around the house if Benita ends up going to jail or something," said Kib.

"Y'all had nothing but hot messes. I think you should just let them decide what they want to do and get with it and do not make any scholar out of them because it ain't there to do. You are draining yourself for nothing. There are a lot of vocational and skill-related programs out there and they can do just about anything a person going to college can do. But they have to do it while they are young and not wait until they are too old." said Latrel.

Kib turned and looked at her and said, "Enough with all that talk. I have a more interesting board game for you..." he said.

It was getting late, and Benita began to worry about Kib.

"Hey, it's me Tang." he said as he spoke with Nadel Rogers from compliance. "I apologize for calling so late but we need to question Benita Drendel. Many of these approval letters were not authorized. We compared them with the doctor's roster.

...

It was late and Latrel shook Kib to wake him up, but he did not respond. She even poured cold water on him, and he didn't move. Latrel did the next best thing. She struggled to get him dressed and she propped him up and put her arm around his and just barely got him to his car. She then called 911 from a pay phone.

"What's your emergency a sleepy woman asked. You are on a recorded line and please don't be so dramatic. This life ain't easy because I have to deal with my kids and sometimes, jivey dude husband." said the 911 operator.

"Focus bitch, I get it life is full of it. But listen I just found a man who was in his car complaining of chest pain and he passed out and I called 911," said Latrel who tried to remain in control.

"Does he have a pulse?" asked the 911 operator.

"No but he got a real nice watch that somebody gon takes if you don't get here quick," said Latrel.

"Can you give me the man's name and address and tell me the location of where you are, and I will send someone over? asked the 911 operator. But one question, will you be there? Because it sounds to me like you know this dick and you got your pay for your hump a rump and now you don't do dishes, so this is all on his wife." said the 911 operator.

"He knew he was driving a phantom when he got in, now I got to go! So y'all get here quick because we are on a recorded line." Latrel gave the woman Kib's name, address, and the motel location of where he was. Latrel hung up the phone and gabbed the rest of her things from the motel and left.

Chapter Twenty-Three

Bren was happy that Teneil was out of school for the summer. Teneil was almost finished with college and wanted to work a full-time job when she got out because more than anything Teneil loved her independence and having her own money. Bren knew this was going to be difficult for Teneil because her father was an informant and working actively with the Klan to oppress what freedom African- Americans would have. Bren had been in conversation with other classmates from where they graduated high school and he found that more often than not many of these people felt ridiculed or betrayed by a school system that was supposed to protect them. Instead, they found themselves with the opposition and having to do work that their parents could not help them with. Many of these people returned to the South because the city was too fast paced for them. Lon should have done the same. As Bren thought to himself. Lon resented young African Americans because they were not born during segregation. Big Troy and Bren knew what Lon was up to. Lon simply wanted to be the house negro and live as though he were Teneils age and not be subject to the prejudices of his age. It was depressing that Bren knew that Lon would be a cannibal of sorts to Teneil because he was so greedy about everything that he took from almost everyone around him just to give them the basics and he then lives his life with all the white women he can handle and fancy food and of course a high paying job without the stress of Aryian people who wanted to oppress African Americans. Secretly, Teneil knew that her father needed to do more and in doing so he put his burdens on her and used another family member to hide his inability but sometimes the pressure she felt was overwhelming. The only thing good about this was that it kept her weight down as her adrenaline from class to class or job kept her going. Lon knew college wasn't easy and it was costly but thanks to the many programs that were out there many people who otherwise would not have been able to go to college were now able to go. But life happens and many people found themselves having to work to care for themselves and or their families, so school was on the back burner for now. Bren was finishing up his night shift at the bank and Big Troy came over to him.

"Yo," he said. "So, like we solid on that ride home?" he asked.

Bren laughed. "I know you don't want to run into Lessy and you shit on yourself when we drove past her the other day."

"I helped you clean the car after you came home with me to change and all. I appreciate your help but my girl, just won't understand if I tell her that I'm still married and up and left and abandoned my kids because I didn't want to be bothered with her. Those kids of mine look just like her and they got her ways, and I wasn't having none of that."

"Then how did y'all get together in the first place?" asked Bren because the way Big Troy talked about Lessy it was as if they had nothing in common.

"It was a family thing. Her family knew mine and they all hung out together and felt it would be good if I and Lessy hooked up. We ran drugs and did all sorts of things including robbery and even numbers. We trusted each other and they felt it was good to keep it in the family and look out for each other. We got along well as friends and could talk to each other. So we got hitched and had the kiddies but not exactly in that order and then we did our things and I began to want to be with other women. I'm a man and I wasn't going to deprive myself of letting all that pu-nay-nay go and watching young howls out there get it all, so I went to go and play it and I got the girl I want to be with now." said Big Troy.

"The girl you got now is my age and you are in your mid-thirties. She must be very naive to think that you have been living on this earth now for this long and don't have a wife or even had one or more children. So how are you gon have a future with her if you ain't being real or even honest? I mean what if Lessy finds you one day after you settle in with this young thang of yours and have kids by her and Lessy come by wanting back child support? How are you gon handle that?"

"The kids of mine are getting big and should be able to do for themselves hopefully before that ever happens. Besides Lessy is smart enough to be working and last I heard she got some company-type job so she doesn't need me no way and if worse comes to worse I will just say that this was all a part of the sacrifices we make for our children so that good will come out of this," said Big Troy who began to sweat and for the most part, he ate himself to the point where he was overweight.

"Look go finish up and wait in the lobby. I will be done in a few. I know you like to leave by a certain time so that you don't see Lessy en-route going to work or any of her family members who can jump out and give you the beat down." said Bren as he giggled.

"Technology has not caught up with people faking their identities. I got me a new birth certificate, a new license, and a new name and I gained the weight so that I look nothing like my former self as I dress differently so that nobody recognizes me," said Big Troy. "I'll see you in a few," he said as he walked back to his workstation.

Bren thought to himself as he thought of his problems and how his mom was handling things with the Klan. She worked long hours, and they had a caretaker come in daily to care for his father who became disabled because he had so many health complications. His mother liked his father to be home and she used him as the black sheep along with Bren so that she could go out and work freely. He felt alone in all of this but knew that Teneil had problems also. She was always preoccupied and busy thinking her way through things that it appeared that even the slightest bit of fun was only on the surface. Teneil loved to laugh and joke but her father Lon hated it. He wanted Teneil to do more as if she were the salvation to others including himself. Lon was as basic as they come. he had no South in him except that of a house negro. The fields were not him and as a child, he vowed to get out of them by avoiding the work or just not being good at it so that he could be sent up North. He knew the ways of the South and they were often biblical since education was not formal for many backs then. They would get the Bible and torture you back and forth until you were born again several times over. It bothered Bren that he knew Teneil was going to have to go through this as Lon would just make a pest of himself by "giving the kids to the parents to punish". Bren knew this was abusive and even for things Teneil had nothing to do with or did not even do. Lon was punishing Teneil for his indiscretions, Quezel, Lon Jr, and of course Jacel's family. Lon was comfortable with the spiritual phrase "Mother" because he could do the bare minimum and leave it at that. Bren hurriedly closed down his workstation and met Big Troy in the lobby and they headed home as Big Troy lay low in the car as Bren was driving.

...

Several hours later the phone rang, and Benita answered it nervously. "Mrs. Drendel," said the woman.

"Yes," answered Benita.

"I am a nurse from Mount Ridge Hospital. Your husband was admitted for a heart attack. He is in very serious condition and in the ICU at the moment." said the nurse.

"Oh, my goodness!" said Benita as she began to cry.

"Can I see him?" she asked.

"Yes, He's in and out of consciousness." said the nurse. "But we must wait until he is stable to try and evaluate him further." said the nurse.

"Kib has really good co-workers, is that who brought him in?" asked Benita.

"Honey, get a clue. It was later in the evening when he got here and from what I understand. He was found in his car outside of a motel. I don't think he was at a rest stop, as a trucker either." said the nurse. "His big boy pants were in a mess as if he had help getting them on and no wife would have her husband looking the way he did when he came in."

Chapter Twenty-Four

"Girl I been trying to call you all damn day. You ain't pick up the phone and I know where Big Troy gonna be later this evening." said Latrina.

"How did you find this out?" asked Latrel. "He dun missed Lil Troy's graduation. The boy gon goes off to a community school on scholarship and he is not around to celebrate his son's milestones or bond with him as he enters manhood. Now, he is some simple shit. But I love him, and I can't seem to get over the feeling of me probably killing him for what he did to me and the kids." said Lessy angrily.

"Now, it's time that you put things into perspective and realize that men and women come together to create life, and sometimes once that is done then the union may end depending on the needs of the children and what obstacles they need to adhere to for their sacrifice and survival. You are doing a good job with the kids Lessy and you have to stop this bitterness. It was Big Troy's loss that he did not want to be bothered with his children." said Latrina as she tried to convince herself of this. We have all been there, the lies, the promises, the abuse, and the neglect. But you know after I got it all together and decided to do for me and be about me and not put it all into a man to make me things changed." said Latrina. "My kids are grown and all and they have learned some of the things that I had to go through when raising them and now they understand."

"All I know is that Lil Troy asks about his father all the time and I ain't got no real answer for him except that maybe one day when he gets old enough which should be about now, he can try to find him. But it bothered me that I couldn't do this for my kids and bring him justice for them. They see his side of the family on occasion, but they never seem to know where Big Troy is and I know they lying to protect his non-child support paying ass and honestly I can't deal with it anymore. It was not their job to raise my kids but the least they could have done was to keep them as part of Big Troy's family or they could have done more to stay in contact." said Lessy tearfully.

"You don't need Big Troy to do that. What you should have done was make it your way to involve your children in the lives of the father's side of the family even if Big Troy was not around. That way somehow or some way they could have found out where Big Troy was without you having to figure things out and threaten people to help you find this man. I have a lead on him and who he hangs out with." said Latrina as she took a deep breath "You interested?" she asked.

"I been waiting since the last time I saw the man walk out the door," said Lessy.

"He's been known to hang around some young dude named Bren," said Latrina.

"That's because all the old people know where his ass is and if I get to talking to them, they will tell me so he doesn't hang around them," said Lessy.

"Well, if you all hang around the same people somebody is bound to find out where Big Troy is staying and tell you where he is," said Latrina. But as I recall as we got older Big Troy seemed distant. He wasn't himself even after you guys got together, he seemed like he wanted something else."

"You mean Big Troy was just putting on pretending to be happy when deep down he wasn't?" asked Lessy.

"That's exactly what I mean," said Latrina as she was trying to get through to Lessy. "Did he ever confide in his feelings to you? asked Latrel.

"No, He always seemed happy-go-lucky, and I never knew he was that unhappy until he never came home," said Lessy who wiped the tears from her face as she hoped to find out where Big Troy was.

"The thing was, is that Big Troy was not happy with his life, and he felt robbed of his youth so to speak by helping out with the drug dealers and having to scrape and get by without getting caught by the police. This took a toll on Big Troy, and he left. As you know most of his childhood was spent working for drug dealers by helping his parents out. That in itself was like a child having to earn his keep to survive. Big Troy learned at an early age that he saw he must do for himself because his parents could not do it alone. This bothered him and made him develop insecurities about his parents and the fact that when they were friends with yours and you decided to keep it in the family so to speak Troy felt like the black sheep and he wanted out of the situation. " said Latrina.

"You know, after Big Troy left, everybody just went off and did their own thing. It was as if something had gone wrong and they had to disband their kinship to get out of something. I even asked my mama about things, and she was vague on the subject and said that I should know more about Big Troy because I had the kids by him and was living with him. She did not help me find him or ask questions about his family. Now that I think about it, she knew more than what she let on and did not want me to know because me and the kids were probably a sacrifice for something." said Lessy as she began to understand. "So, it wasn't all Big Troy's fault?" she said.

"No girl, I think that his family made him do what he did as a disbandment to what they were into to avoid jail time and in the process, they made him leave you also," said Latrina. "But he was unhappy with how things were going, and he hated to put on a facade. So when the time came for his family to do what they had to do to avoid jail time Big Troy was the answer and Big Troy was also ready to leave them behind. He was saving himself and you along with the children. said Latrina. Latrina knew Big Troy wanted more out of life and he wanted to regain the youth he missed out on by having to help his parents.

Lessy was not convinced. Big Troy could have called her or sent word to her through family that this was the issue, and she could have gone with him. She didn't buy the fact that Big Troy left to fulfill a family obligation with the law by using religion as a way out and he willingly accepted it. Lessy also didn't buy the fact that Big Troy didn't have a choice in the matter, and he was to do what he was told or else. Lessy grew up with people who came from single-parent homes and didn't think much of it, but she also didn't want it to happen to her especially since her parents were married for so long. It was unfair and they seemed to gloat about her unhappiness. Lessy was ready to take things or matters into her own hands and was tired of living a life of someone else's deceit. She had grown cold and certainly dated other men throughout, but she never found a man like Big Troy and she didn't want another. Lessy wanted to hear it from Big Troy, and she wanted to know if he left because he wanted a younger version of her which he finally has and so that he could live the life of a young person without any responsibility such as raising a family. She knew that Big Troy was in it with his family, and he kept in contact with them secretly. Lessy was angry and despite Latrina's attempts to console her and make her focus on something else the pain that Lessy felt was unbearable she needed to let Big Troy know exactly how she felt and had decided to kill him. She tried to remain calm in an effort for Latrina to tell her where Big Troy would be.

"So where can I at least look at him?" asked Lessy.

"Well, he gained some weight and looks preppy so you would probably walk past him, but you may recognize his voice. Now, he and Bren are going to have dinner and drinks at the Ho-So-Ho gig in Molawi. There's a section of that town that has quite an active nightlife with clubs, movie theaters, and trendy restaurants where young people frequent the area along with people going through mid-life issues. Big Troy and Bren go there to hang out and perhaps if you saw how husky, fat, and not even good-looking he is, you are going to change your mind about all of this. I'm telling you. The man looks way different and you gon says, I'm so glad he left me. I think it's time you saw him get this irritable pain away from you so that you can move on with your life and not be in the dumps and let this prevent you from finding love again. I really mean it girl you got to get out there." said Latrina.

"How you know they gon be there tonight?" asked Lessy.

"My sources are never wrong," said Latrina

"Thank you. I will see what I can do," said Lessy as she hung up the phone.

She walked into the room where Lil Troy was half asleep and she tapped him, and he woke up.

"Hey ma," he said sleepily.

"Want to go see your daddy?" asked Lessy.

"You mean he called after all this time? Did he ask about me? He must have known that I graduated from high school." asked Lil Troy as he became excited.

"Not exactly," said Lessy quietly.

"Then how we gon get to see him if you didn't talk to the man?" asked Lil Troy.

"I'll tell you on the way. Get up and get ready and you can bring your friend with you if you like," said Lessy.

"Where are we going?" asked Lil Troy.

"We going to the Ho-So-Ho gig," said Lessy.

Within an hour or so Lessy and Lil Troy were going to pick up Lil Troy's friend and they were driving down the busy street of Molawi until Lil Troy found a parking space he could squeeze into. They got out and saw a crowd waiting outside the Ho-So-Ho gig. Lessy clenched her handgun tightly in her bag as she spotted Big Troy and his girlfriend.

"Aww isn't that nice," Lessy said to herself as she held onto her gun. She wanted to shoot him right there, but people were moving around and blocking her view and she did not want to shoot an innocent bystander.

"Mama, do you see him?" asked Lil Troy anxiously.

"Uh, no," she said calmly I think maybe we should wait until we get inside.

Lil Troy's friend saw a cabana a few stores down, "I'm gonna get me a drink." she said colorfully as she waltzed out of the line and a few stores down. Lil Troy and Lessy held their place in line as they moved closer and closer to getting inside the Ho-So-Ho gig. Lessy watched as Big Troy and his girlfriend entered the So-Ho-So gig. Several minutes later Lil Troy's friend came back with a tray full of drinks and they waited a few minutes longer. They entered to Ho-So-Ho gig and Lessy nervously looked around for Big Troy and saw him seated at a table with his girlfriend, Bren, and a few other people. They were eating appetizers and laughing. The server brought them to a table not too far from where Big Troy was sitting. Lessy smiled and excused herself from the table.

"Where are you going?" asked Lil Troy.

"Right over there..." she said as Lil Troy as he and his friend opened their menus.

Lessy walked over to Big Troy and pulled out a gun from her bag and shot him several times.

"Oh, shit, you must be Lessy. The woman this fool that just slumped over said he divorced many years ago!" yelled Big Troy's girlfriend.

"You are correct, but don't worry you are not in jeopardy. You one of them young dumb bitches." said Lessy

Big Troy's girlfriend decided not to argue as she looked around and realized that customers had scattered out of the restaurant and others had ducked under their tables.

Lil Troy got up and saw what his mother had done and said, "Dang mama I was just looking at the menu and all you wanted to order was a hit!"

Chapter Twenty-Five

"Uh, Hey Mr. Deivers, It's Lon Roner give me a call when you get my message," said Lon as he hung up the phone.

Mr. Deivers was sitting at his desk the entire time but didn't answer because he liked to hear Lon's voice. It was usually desperate and willing to almost do anything to date someone like Elkin. He also didn't want to do anything by way of business fundraising. He didn't know how to take computer programming to the next level and certainly didn't want to be relegated to developing programs for those who had mental challenges. It was true that Lon has boasted himself into saying that this was all he was about, but it was a lie. Developing computer programs to work took a lot of time and energy. It also took passion, patience, and an honest love of seeing that a program could be beneficial. Lon didn't want to be involved in finding people to do this type of work. He knew it would pay a lot of money down the line, but he knew if he talked a good game he would be able to work and do the programming by working with groups of people instead of him having to sit alone and develop programs himself. He didn't want to use Teneil because it would enable her to earn a lot of money and if that were to happen, he could no longer use her as a pawn instead he and Mr. Deivers had another idea.

Mr. Deivers dialed Lon's number at work and Lon answered the phone anxiously.

"Hello Lon, it's Mr. Deivers I just received your call. Have you thought over our plan?" asked Mr. Deivers.

"Why yes. I think it's an excellent idea. Some will fall through the cracks if we don't handle it this way. There are students in the regular school system that don't fit into your program because they are not disabled like Lon Jr., but they have a disability that prevents them from learning and applying the information. Your program focuses on people who cannot learn the information or task. You want me and a few others to take it to the next level and put people together who are reasonably bright like Teneil and put them with people who cannot apply the information. In another words the information is there they just don't know what to do with it. Teneil can basically do most of the work and the others that are hired who have this application issue will be extremely limited in the workplace, but they can work as long as someone like Teneil can do the heavy lifting." said Lon Roner as he smiled.

"We often think that using religion is the way of the world and serves our purpose and gives them one. Teneil is a person of the field, and she will grow and acclimate to her surroundings and become a part of what we want to establish in our modern-day society," said Mr. Deivers.

"Her education will prepare her for this and make her tough enough to do a myriad of things and not worry about working in a group or with a group of people. Because we are going to arrange this in clusters and pair people together," said Lon quietly. "I find that when you have large groups of people and everybody doing the same thing or even something different when you compare the quality of work or need them to handle something alone it is found that what is learned cannot be applied thus making that individual ineffective in the workplace. Then people start to talk and complain, and that person is not able to work in certain situations. Honestly, nobody likes to be looked at as a problem or even someone who has to go on disability because people will frown upon it and see it as a stigma. Children who have superior status should not be looked upon with a stigma."

"She must be able to handle who she is and her role in America. Lon as a person of the house, you must define her role for her and not let her make her own decisions or chart her life course. If this happens, we will have consequences and fears about not being in control or superior. This is important to our foundation and earthy purpose. Teneil may be free, but she must work within the certain confines of our existence as we know it to be. Lon we are counting on you to make this possible do I have your word?" asked Mr. Deivers.

"Yes, yes you do. I understand these people hold more of a superior value than Teneil and we do not want them to fall through the cracks and for them not to do so people like Teneil will hold them up," said Lon as he agreed. "Teneil seems to be coming along fine and I will do all I can so that our plans for superiority and continued economic growth.

"Good day, Lon," said Mr. Deivers as he hung up the phone.

Lon was ecstatic and relieved that he would not be responsible for writing computer programs or other educational learning designed for computers. Lon just wanted relief from the responsibility of raising a family and sought to console himself after he and Elkin divorced. Lon never forgave the sacrifice he had to make to preserve his life because being married to Elkin would have cost him dearly. Besides, it would help Drecker get the help she needs to move along and be one of the privileged. He had to devise a way to find out what Teneil was going to do with herself and thwart her plans, dreams, and goals in barter for what he wanted her to do because he certainly was going to stop laying up with other women and he was not doing to do all-nighters in writing programs for computers. he felt punished by having children in this condition and he certainly wasn't going to punish himself anymore by having to learn how to create an educational computer program. That was out of the question.

Teneil, on the other hand, was suffering she thought about Lon Jr. every day and she could not say his name without crying. She knew her parents had given up hope on him and were preoccupied with things that for the most part didn't concern them. But she knew all along this was a way to pass the buck. She knew to live in a group home and having staff to care for people like Lon Jr. would cost money. And she feared that the government would not provide the necessary funds to house, feed, and care for these children adequately. She had to come up with a plan to get people with the money to donate so that Lon Jr.

and others like him would be cared for properly. Teneil knew this was something her father and mother could not handle. They were basic parents and she had to convince herself that they couldn't do much more than that and wished that she had different parents because they expected more out of her than what they could do. This was unfair to Teneil because everybody else would be out living and enjoying their life and Teneil would be the sacrificial lamb. Teneil decided to rise to the occasion, although she had no idea how to do this. Teneil hoped one day that somebody would hear her pleas for help and develop a system of selling the idea to those who can fulfill the product and create the sale to provide for those who are not able to do it for themselves. She found her father Lon a tyrant who always wanted more as if he was so capable of doing such things. But he wasn't he wasn't your typical group worker who did just enough to get by and her mother was no teacher, after getting Valdena Plantation to put the squeeze on her in school, it was as if she was doing homework for two people. Jacel Roner and Valdena Plantation went to high school together. If they could be white both of them would. She got tired of hearing the excuses of being twice as good. That nonsense was just so that somebody like her could do the work and somebody like Quezel didn't have to. Teneil knew she had to plan accordingly so that she would be able to do all that she dreamed of doing and to help Lon Jr. He needed her because his parents were not able to handle what lay ahead. What was an issue was that her father never had any friends and seemed to like to conversate with whites who were not so nice people to people like Teneil. The doorbell rang and Teneil answered it. She looked out and saw it was Bren Chopper.

Chapter Twenty-Six

Benita Drendel knew things were closing in on her. Her husband Kib had suffered a heart attack that left him needing her constant help and Wendor seemed to not want to finish college as Marlie struggled through. "This was probably for the best.", she thought to herself. Without having to worry about paying for college tuition she could get the girls to get a job and help her with the household expenses. Kib was receiving disability, but it was not nearly enough to cover the bills and to avoid being caught in the letter scandal Benita felt it best to resign from her position. Kib lay in bed most of the time as people from the Klan organization checked in with them and brought food and other things to defray the cost of Kib's medical bills. Benita was angry with Kib because she felt that he failed her as a husband. The job of a husband is to provide for the family. She knew the days of chivalry were gone and women had to get out and do it for themselves and she almost felt ashamed to depend on Kib or blame him anymore. The jobs out there were often demanding and did not pay enough for the average family to live off on. She wished she had a job like Kib's but she needed to clout or probably the education. Benita even thought to herself that if she could contact Lon, she knew he would help her. Lon was the house negro that would go above and beyond to do anything for those that looked nothing like him and seek salvation from those that did look like him by throwing them under the bus. Without that extra money, they would probably have to sell the house or take out a reverse mortgage which is something of a last resort, but it would give her time to plan her next move. She went through Kib's phone book and decided to give Lon a call.

"Lon?" Benita asked reluctantly.

"Hey, Benita I was just thinking about Lon. How is he doing? I got some information that he needs to know, or you could probably pass it along." said Lon.

"Which is?" asked Benita.

"I got word that the networks are aggressively pursuing college graduates and I find it unfair if whites are learning impaired them many of these jobs will go to Black people and that is a reverse discrimination. You know things Black people are always complaining about." said Lon.

Benita laughed because the things came out of Lon's mouth you would think he was white. "You mean because they are hiring them only because they are black and not as if you were to hire a person only because they are white." said Benita.

"Exactly," said Lon. "The problem becomes is that they are putting people in positions to have careers as a result. The mental capabilities have changed for people and when there a job that probably requires a certain intellect and they cannot get it from whites they hire blacks as an attraction and pay them much less," said Lon.

"Well, if they do these jobs for next to nothing then what is all the fuss about?" asked Benita because she knew that the standard of living would not be so good and they would still have struggled as would a white person with an issue in learning.

"But we're supposed to be equal and that is not putting everyone black and white on an equal level," argued Lon.

Benita thought to herself and realized that Lon was about as useless as Kib. She knew that you have to compare apples to apples. It was as if they had forgotten that there are mentally impaired blacks, and they are not including them in on this. Benita then realized that the Klan would go to every length to see to it that slavery or oppression would remain in effect.

"Now Kib is in no position to take the information I have for him, so I'm giving it to you as needed," said Lon.

"Ok, so when I go to my meetings as such, I will pass this on but..." said Benita.

Lon began to interrupt Benita by giving her the names of people with great potential to change the world as African Americans and he did not want whites to be threatened by them as whites felt the need to only keep an appointed house negro such as Lon in terms of being gainfully employed. Regression and perhaps job reassignment would equal things for blacks and whites.

"Fine that will be our continued goal," said Benita. "Now, Lon I have a favor to ask of you and I'm only asking because you have been a solid informant and have been good to the fact that you are loyal to our understanding of superiority and to preserve our legacy in slavery. We appreciate all your efforts and hope that you will continue to be a valuable resource to it all. Now having said that because Lon is on disability, I need to work within the salary range of Lon's to maintain this household. Now, if you can't help me then perhaps you may have to put your house for sale so that we can be on an equal level." said Benita in a serious manner.

Lon laughed, "What you trying to tell me is that if I don't help you, I am going to lose my house negro status. Not a chance. But I did offer you Teneil so that she won't own one because she is one of those people that we don't want to see as a common threat, and I thought that would even things out." said Lon.

"Lon, I need help now. I can't wait until we decide to have them in the oppressed job positions," said Benita.

"I thought you were working and doing pretty good for yourself." Said Lon.

"Kib made all the money and only spent a fraction of it on what we needed to survive. The rest of his money went to sluts, motels and liquor. As a result of his heart attack the medical bills are piling up and I did some things to make extra money and things have caught up with me somewhat." said Benita tearfully. I can just hang it all up together and move in with my mother. It would be tight, but she would be able to see the kids more and I would not have to worry about everything it takes to have a home and sometimes you wonder if it's worth it."

"I suppose I can talk to my superior and have you fill in for Kib if they are hiring. But that would mean that you would have to work for Blue Onx permanently. I thought that you loved working for Trinity Insurance Company?" asked Lon

"I did but those bastards don't pay enough, and I was just thinking of a way to earn money and also help other companies out and now this audit comes along and ruins everything and makes it such that with the introduction of new software I won't be able to do a letter on the side to make money and people are going to find out about our illegal doings," said Benita.

"So, I take it that you resigned, already?" asked Lon.

"I'm getting it together now so that I can give it to them and leave with no questions asked," said Benita.

"You know that in some instances to avoid being charged with a crime or having to return the money to the company they may not pay you for vacations or time you have left, severance pay, or even your pension fund. They may take all of that from you and even refuse you unemployment. Benita, you have to be willing to accept this to get out from under the mess you are in. Now, while you are doing this I will talk to my superiors and see if you can be of use at Blue Onx, that way you will not have too much of a drastic lifestyle change and you won't kick me out of my abode as a result." said Lon as Benita laughed

"Ok, that sounds like a plan." she said. "Now I have to get going because he's expecting to see me at the hospital, and he is anxious to get out of there." she said "They are going to try rehab later in the week. I just don't think that he's ready." said Benita reluctantly.

"I know, Kib only likes to move one part of his body and if it ain't that then you're going to have a time with him as a result." said Lon.

"Should I contact his mistress and have her help him and then divorce Kib and get an entitlement to his pension because he will have to admit to cheating?" asked Benita. You know I did not understand until now why men were so cheap and often spend money frivolously and never saved."

"So when it came time to divorce they had no money or assets to give to the former wife and it frees them from financial strain and burden. Kib is not the imp that you think he is. Now let me get going so that I can get ahold of somebody so that you can have a job quite soon after you leave Trinity Health Insurance," said Lon.

"Ok," said Benita. "I will give you a call in a day or two and also let you know how Kib is coming along," she said.

Benita got up and got her things ready and went to get a few things to take to Kib she looked out and saw two police officers coming to her front door.

"What on earth could have happened?" asked Benita as she opened the door.

The two officers looked up and one of them asked, "Are you Benita Drendel?"

"Yes," Benita answered.

"You have to come with us." said the other officer.

"Why," asked Benita.

"You are being changed with Medicaid fraud along with several others. Now, come with us and we will discuss this at the police station." said the officer.

Gan Pouter who lived next door to Benita was on vacation and watched as the police officers took Benita out of her house.

"Hey Benita, anything I can help you with?" asked Gan.

"Yes, I need to talk to a lawyer. I'm being railroaded," yelled Benita as they shoved her into the police car.

"I'll be right over to the police station," he said.

Gan ran back into the house and left his female companion on the sofa.

"Oh, so now we doing this?" she asked.

"Doing what?" he asked as he hurried to get dressed.

"We were just having fun." said the woman.

"You took my nut and now I need money to keep the lights on," explained Gan.

"I suggested that you turn them out while we were at it but you refused." said the woman.

"Look, you can't be too careful these days. I like to see what I'm getting into. Now, you can go or stay here. The choice is up to you. But I work for the court, and I see this as a case I can get her to cop a plea and I can get paid and be on my way." said Gan who was an attorney.

"I still have one other question?" asked the woman as Gan was going out the door.

"Make it snappy. What is it?" asked Gan.

"Did I get the job?" asked the woman.

"Was that your resume you just handed me? Babe look at the competition that's out there. Uh, let me get back to you. I will be there in no time." said Gan.

Chapter Twenty-Seven

Several years had gone by and after many delays, Lessy was found guilty of murder even as she pleaded insanity of having to raise a family by herself. Bren felt a sense of relief although he missed his friend Big Troy who looked out for him and mentored him along the way. At Big Troy's funeral, he met Rezel Telon who he kept in contact with but eventually became very sick.

"I'm gonna miss you," said Teneil who sat outside her house as Bren came by to say goodbye.

"Yeah, the South is where the job has gone so I guess I will go with it." said Bren.

"Can't you find another job within the company?" asked Teneil.

"Not one that pays this good and will not require me to have all kinds of sophisticated schooling," said Bren.

"Look what good it did me," said Teneil angrily.

"I know girl, it's been hard for you but one day your elder's ignorance will catch up to them. I, I just don't believe in it," she said tearfully.

Bren watched Teneil helplessly as he knew that Teneil was on her own, but he knew that what comes around goes around one day Lon and the others would get their comeuppance. Lon was like a big kid who didn't want any responsibility and wanted his life back before he met the reality of racism. He was forced to divorce Elkin and leave his daughter Drecker because he did not have the sacrificial strength to stay with them. Racism was like a disease that eroded people and would take a toll on one's mind, body, and soul. Teneil was bitter as she questioned the point of civil rights because it just seemed to her that black men wanted were white women and homosexuality. Much of this behavior existed through slavery but was never talked about as people were freed some were not subjected to such treatment and there were some who enjoyed it and decided to use it as barter, exchange, or commodity.

Teneil knew she had the answer, and it was because slavery had created a corrupt existence of religion of people and it was continued through oppression.

"I'm gonna miss the big city but I like areas that are spread out and country," said Bren.

Teneil laughed, "I doubt that this is something I could ever get used to."

"Teneil, Rezel Telon knew your father while they were in the Navy together told me that they had to escape the racism of the South but at the same time, the North proved too fast for them. Sure, they dropped slaves off all over the place but with integration, you'll find an epistle or work grind that takes a toll if you're one of those that they use for sacrifice. Somehow the body adapts to the speed of things, and they work with the fierceness of the city, so when you enslave people over time it becomes nothing more than work. The sacrifice or using one as a sacrifice has manifested to that of the Spirit and God measures that to give his vengeance. Bren continued, "Lon came up with the idea along with your grandmother that if they took people and put them in areas that they don't like to be in or jobs that they don't want and they would cause a huge recession as a result of all of this as more of a modern third world existence."

"And they want to use this is a conspiracy to try and slow down the progression of AIDS in people?" asked Teneil

"Yup!" said Bren.

"Ok, so this is a concept that they were creating all along, and now that they have things the way they want them this is the only way that they conjured up to avoid the wrath of God. Honestly, with this disease, God had his helpers to spread this thing along as a lesson to people but this shit has gotten out of hand and it's causing damn near everybody to sacrifice. Some sooner than others." said Bren as he looked around.

Teneil always questioned the existence of God. It was like living spiritually in a cruel world where every joke around you was played on you. Teneil did not get out much and Bren knew the real reason was that many people were sinners who seek others for their salvation. Bren hated to see Teneil being treated this way but she was surrounded by ignorance. People didn't want to take responsibility for themselves or their transgressions. It was easier to go to a confession booth and have the man put the burden on someone else. The Church was misled and a lot of that was due to the abuse and power of ministers, and fathers who were all human and were the intercessor or communication to the spirit of God but abused their authority to the point that they created a choir of hell instead of heaven. "I supposed living this way would make one appreciate the thought of heaven and others are packed and ready to go to hell. It had been years since she was happy about something the pressure and uncertainty mounted as she knew her father Lon chose to play instead of work and her mother did not know what to do about any of it but to put the burden on Teneil. Life was changing for Teneil as she wanted to challenge her theory of good works as a way to communicate with the creator. Teneil thought for a moment and then realized something. The notion of being twice as good as she thought about the wrath of God and how he plays a part in avenging humans by mocking their existence. Whites often tell blacks that they have to be twice as good and this is the way God works. Faith without works is dead. Faith is one good and work is the second good so if you don't do both then you are not twice as good in the book of God. Teneil so wanted to prove people were wrong by using other people as cannibals and acting without regard for human beings. But, that was the thought of a southerner named Lon who was ignorant and didn't know any more than what he learned when he left the South. He would work with groups of people and then use somebody as the black sheep without them knowing it. This was how he got away clean and didn't have to do any techy work that he promised or made it appear that he was going to do when chatting with Mr. Deivers or Valdena Plantation. Lon had it all planned out and he could just regress and sit back, and no one would ever suspect that he did very little for his family except for providing the basics such as three meals and a cot and then abusing them when he did anything else. She knew Lon hated his people and used them for his sacrifice including her and even those lighter than him he just threw them into the mix to get as far as he could until he could get back into the graces of people like Elkin. He feared being around white people alone because he knew that being from the South would make him a target so he played it cool and planned everything carefully until he was able to use Teneil the way he wanted. However, Teneil had another idea. Sure she wanted Lon Jr. to be in a good home because she could not provide for him but she hated the fact that Lon abused her by having her do all of the work and putting her in a situation as he and Mr. Deivers planned this out carefully. Mr. Deivers knew that if Teneil was going to pay for the ignorance of others then they would try to put her on welfare but if that didn't work then using a learning-disabled person in the workplace would suffice because it would serve the purpose of racism, sin, and salvation. Teneil was out of tears and was ready to put her use of good work to the test. She gave Bren a pat on the back as she said goodbye to him and began to think outside of the box. "These people have no God in them.", she thought to herself and that was their downfall they relied on others for their salvation and that was not fair because it was as if there was a fully grown adult who never took responsibility for what they did and that was going to change one way or another.

Jacel Roner sat as she was talking to Quezel and they were looking at Teneil funny.

"What's up?' she asked.

"So we heard Bren is moving South, so what are you going to do with the rest of your life?" asked Jacel.

"I think I have enough to keep me busy, so I don't think I need the company too much," said Teneil.

Quezel and Jacel seemed puzzled. Teneil always seemed so outgoing but ever since they did the life swap with her so that her father Lon, and other relatives could avoid responsibility for their transgressions Teneil knew that hanging out was no longer an option and she didn't want to help sinners by being out on the street so she decided to revert to her homebody self and get to work if she was going to be twice as good as the creator asked of people. This was going to take a lot of work and time and there was no time to hang out and do things that strayed from her mission.

"I have to get going, I got things to do." said Quezel sarcastically.

Quezel quickly left the house and Jacel seemed to be at a loss for words because she could never tell Teneil why she was having her do this. Lon ruled things along with his pathic slob of a mother-in-law but what could she do? The church allowed the elders to take over in times of crisis as this allowed people to do what they wanted because they had their sacrifices in place and they assumed that no one would be in contact with the creator because his good works were some kind of school that many refused to be a part of because it requires a lot of work and energy to be on the frequency of the creator so that the creator would do unto others as they did unto her. She had to prove to the creator that she was worthy and willing to do the work. Her job was nothing to brag about or even be proud of, but she knew it was useless because it was a confession of the sins of others. It was an awful position to be in and if she could contact the creator, he would avenge what those were doing and make them pay for what they did. It was time that people stopped using others as cannibals and if they can't shit then they should get off the can and stop using it to cause problems for others and making it seem like they do so much or more than what they actually do and get paid for things and then put down others who do work and have them suffer by making less. This was done to make whites superior and to make Lon in his narcissism feel as if he is the house negro that he wanted to be.

Chapter Twenty-Eight

Life had changed for Kib since his heart attack. He worked for a few years and was then put back on disability because he suffered a mild stroke which caused him to have several other problems. Benita was given probation for her role in the letter scheme at Trinity Insurance company and she instead found work as an assistant manager in a food chain of stores. She liked the fact that she gave orders and was given the perks of discounted food. There were times when she saw to it that she got it for free but that was Benita and she was going to survive no matter what. She wasn't angry with Kib for cheating on her because Kib was a man and as she saw that man was still a beast and will do what it does. What did anger her about Kib was that he like a lot of other men neglected their families. They treat them like prisoners with three meals and a cot and if they give you any more than that then you are going to pay for it. A wife and kids were seen as free labor and sacrificial labor as far as a man was concerned and she was sure that some women who took on the role of the man in a household thought the same way. It was as if that man was God and you worked and toiled for pennies just for him to live in his self-described comfort and have his pleasure. Her suffering was over in that Kib was not able to have the dalliances with other women that he had in the past. His body was ravaged by the abuse he put it through over many years as he would often stay up very late, drink, smoke, and have as many women as he wanted all while Benita struggled to raise their children and find money to pay the bills. It simply was not enough, she knew she would soon have to move as she waited for the girls to move out on their own. But still, there were the Klan ties that had to be attended to and Kib often had meetings at his home because he could not get out very often and with the trouble Benita got into she didn't want to be seen in an area that would link her to Klan people if the police ever showed up. Benita felt lucky that Kib got sick when he did because that was what gave her some leniency in avoiding jail time. It was a woman's purpose to care for her man and she supposed that was what kept her from going behind bars.

Trinity Health Insurance was failing and sinking deeper and deeper into debt. Many subscribers were not paying their premiums and many people were disgruntled. They did not understand socialized medicine and its adaptation of it in today's modern world. Trinity Health Insurance was secretly underwritten by a dioceses in that to be properly diagnosed and treated was like walking the plank with the father, son, and the holy spirit. Those who didn't feel they had an obligation to themselves by caring for themselves properly, were subjected to the worst doctors, and those who didn't know what they were doing. For many, their illness was discovered due to a self-diagnosis and many visits to different doctors and by that time the illness had spread. Insurance companies were tired of paying exorbitant health costs to those people who refused to care for themselves. Several health insurance companies went out of business and others simply had to merge to continue providing health care options to people. Trinity Health Insurance was secretly sending a message to many of its employees and members that it was time to take care of themselves. There were more bad or incompetent doctors than good ones and because medical school was rigorous not many people had the talent or ability to survive the brutal classes and testing they would endure throughout their careers. With that in mind Trinity being a managed care organization was limited to what its members could choose and a healthcare provider. It was not a law that every doctor had to accept particular health insurance. But it was a rule that if they were to be a part of a managed care organization they had to be willing to accept Medicaid. Many doctors despised doing so because it meant that they did not take in the upper crust of society. Doctors liked the commercial insurance that paid well as this would enable doctors to order as many tests and procedures on a patient without the insurance company denying the procedures or refusing to pay out. Everybody was cutting down and insurance companies were reviewing procedures and the necessity of them to avoid fraud, waste, and abuse from medical professionals. This was what led Benita to do what she did because if she didn't send some of the business to other companies they would go out of business. Benita questioned the Medicaid managed care business model. It was just as if they took Medicaid and created a working enterprise that funded itself by having health insurance that those who were slightly above poverty could pay into. But at what cost? If those from Essential Plans were to subsidize the healthcare for the Medicaid managed care plans there would still be a deficit owed from the insurance company because the Trinity role model of father, son, and holy spirit often resulted in people finding out about illnesses or diagnoses too late and as a result, it became costly to the insurance company. The business model had to change for health insurance companies to survive. Health insurance was now divided into rich and poor and there was no in-between. It was a doctor's right to refuse a patient in that they did not accept the health insurance plan. Health insurance needed an overhaul and Benita knew that Trinity was based on a religious concept in that you went to the man in confession and man as the intercessor went to God and God would send in his son, the spirit. But God helps those who help themselves and as such there were no answers for many or salvation because people were not doing anything to help themselves. Instead, they went to others for their salvation. It was as if an experiment was being played out and the poor and those not too far off from it were subjected to the experiment. "If people are paying in to a plan that is just a beefed up version of Medicaid then why can't they pay into a Medicare plan and be covered under commercial insurance thus giving more options to providers? This made much more sense." Benita said to herself.

Kib had awakened from one of his long naps.

"Benita!" he yelled.

"Yes!" she answered.

"I'm hungry but I don't feel like going downstairs to eat," he said.

"I will bring your food up to you, meanwhile we have to sell this place. It's costing us more than we can afford. Besides, if we find an apartment you won't have to worry too much about climbing the stairs." said Benita.

"Where are we going to go that will allow us to live rather cheaply? You lost your gig with your stupid ass by your little side hustle. Now, I have to play sicker than I am to keep you out of jail." he yelled.

"Well!" snapped Benita, "If someone gave me enough to pay for all the bills and provided as he should have. This whole thing would have never happened." she said.

"Look you could have gotten two jobs and not spent so much time and energy bilking the other one," said Kib.

"Well, you can try to work a part-time one and stop giving the physical therapist a hard time," said Benita.

"Look, I'm afraid to go anywhere with you and I certainly don't want to work part-time knowing that the other idiots who got harsher sentencing from all of this may have it in for you. If I go walking out with you and I look as though I can manage myself, then they're going to say ok we want you to do a certain amount of jail time. Benita, we have to play it cool until all of this blows over." pleaded Kib.

"Stace and Devou got out of jail and are trying to get it together I just wanted to keep in contact with them more," said Benita as she was finally upstairs in their bedroom.

"Now is not the time. They may be trying to put this all on you so that they can clean their criminal record. Benita, you've all done wrong and I'm not going to let you go down like this." said Kib.

"You mean you feel guilty about not providing for our family enough all of these years and now you're willing to protect me from going to jail.?" said Benita as she watched Kib get up slowly.

"Benita, I don't think we should suffer and no more than we have already done." Kib then picked up his cane.

"I thought you weren't going downstairs," asked Benita.

"I wasn't but we still have to be briefed on things of a Klan nature, Supposedly they got Teneil and others like her working hard to be able to work alongside those with learning disabilities, and along with it I suppose they will use her for the overhead for those who make money by other means," said Kib.

"Such as the life of the Black one," said Benita.

"For some reason, I don't think this is going to work. All this does is keep Lon as the house negro so that he does not have to do any heavy lifting. He won't have to do any work to generate money or raise money for Lon Jr. He will just use Teneil and that think tank brain of hers to do so and whatever else she comes up with creatively." said Kib.

Kib then limped into the kitchen carefully and looked out the window to make sure that they were not being followed. He wanted to thank the attorney next door for helping them through all of this by making Benita look like a struggling working mother who was put into the position by doing what she did to keep her job. Besides he liked the women he saw go in and out of his home. "Come on get dinner really and get them snacks out so when we have this meeting we can get our progress reports and go from there." said Kib.

"I have a new proposition to overhaul health care and I think it's needed. I know Trinity Health insurance relies on the people to get the message, but the problem is that they are getting the wrong message and as a result, the spirit avenges what evils were done and health insurance companies either go out of business or raise costs as a result."

"Which is?" asked Kib.

"We need to be able to pay into Medicare. For those under 65 years old, there needs to be health insurance offered under Medicare that will allow those people who are working to pay into those plans thus increasing the monies contributed by the trust that Medicare is currently funded under. This way if you have the Medicare 21-29 plan, Medicare 30-39 plan, Medicare 40-49 plan, Medicare 50-59 plan, and the Medicare 60 plus plan you have a trust that is earning money based on the premiums paid by the members so that the company will stay solvent in turbulent times. Now Medicaid will still exist, but it will remove the strain on the government because there is no trust to support the program and as a result physicians and facilities get reimbursed less. So what we need to do is to offer more options for workers which include more participating providers. For certain age groups, there will be a third-party authorization review mechanism so that doctors are not abusing the system but with a plan like this members will not be so dissatisfied with their health insurance knowing that they are covered under an insurance backed by a trust. Managed care cannot continue to exist without changing hands and transition insecurity due to being insolvent and not meeting up to regulatory standards because a company is not able to be sustainable. The trust of the Medicare and those members that pay into it is what is needed as the investment and continuation for the future. The reason why these Medicaid plans are failing is that there was no trust and the money that was paid into it was quickly depleted due to illness and the lack of participating physicians. In that business model, people went elsewhere by staying with regular Medicaid and sought treatment at health centers and clinics."

"Benita, you are a woman of redemption!" said Kib as he hugged her while she prepared dinner.

Chapter Twenty-Nine

Lon Roner had the life he had and he was miserable. He was born into a race and class of non-privileged. He made the most of it by being the house-negro at any company that would have him and by using Teneil as a pawn. "Why not?" he would say to himself, she was cute and smart to the where she would be an asset to many. Lon felt that would be a waste if she married because she would only belong to one as opposed to being used by many. Abuse is abuse, you can be abused by a husband which many women were no strangers to or you can be isolated and rejected or singled out by your race which was also abusive. Teneil thought about this and choose to walk the plank. She found solace in the Bible and spent many a night putting her life in perspective. "They say, God, don't make mistakes." That is because God wasn't a student. He gave life lessons and saw to it that one suffered through them when he put them to the test to fulfill his promise as life's lesson.

Teneil wrote books and created electronic music this helped her focus on the spiritual conversation she enjoyed having and the insight that she was provided with. She hated her father Lon because she figured out that he wanted to live the life he wanted and she supposed he wasn't ballsy enough or wasn't man enough to be on his own to handle the undertaking it would take to do this. Lon Jr. has been out of his Clear Horizon program for about two years and Mr. Deivers had been calling Lon like a bitch in heat. She knew that her father Lon was unhappy with who he was and was in many a way ashamed and wanted to fit in with white society. Racism was alive and not making anybody well. Lon wanted or wished he could have stayed married to Elkin and expanded their family. But if Lon could not be the house negro then he would not date a woman outside of his race because the sacrifices are way too much. Being disliked by Elkin's side of the family and the possibility of having kids that looked like him. They would suffer the same fate and be challenged as he would and for Lon that was too much to bear. Being a house-negro was a challenge and he had to be on the lookout for anyone who wanted to do the same thing so that he would be the only one. Lon hated people who looked like him because they were his competition and he knew how to get rid of them. He would go South on them and use the fact that they have another calling or purpose in life. Lon knew that once he and a few others like him Klan'ed up to the white men as informants they would be few high-paying jobs for people that looked like him and this made whites feel secure and put blacks at the bottom as though they were never to rise as a result of continued oppression often at the hands of their own people.

By this time Teneil was working in a medical office which was brutal. Teneil was blackballed and made to walk the plank as though she were not accepted by her own. "Thank God, I'm a loner," said Teneil to herself as she was very busy with work. She was a person of color who was educated and they saw her color as a handicap but her intelligence as a commodity. Talk about your people doing something to her she was getting it from the Hindi folks, Klan's folks, and the mentally disabled and made no money to take care of herself to be on her own. She had a melting pot of bigotry but that would not stop Teneil Roner. Besides her training ground was her family and those who were acquaintances. Her family fair-weathered her and only went to her when times got rough. In this instance, it was Jacel's brother who was out there and now needed someone for his salvation. Lon Roner felt this was the perfect time to become a cannibal of sorts towards Teneil, if he did this he could help Jacel's brother and himself by having just the salvation he needed to find someone like Elkin to have an affair with. And that was how Teneil came to work in a doctor's office. He and Mr. Deivers found day programs for people to help people like Wendor and Quezel. For Jacel's brother, and himself Lon bartered Teneil into working in the medical profession. This meant that Teneil would go through just as much abuse at work as she did at home. Teneil continued to work and educate herself and write. During this time technology and computers had come a long way. Even if she didn't talk very much she enjoyed the atmosphere online because she did what she liked to do best learn without anyone bothering her or having to do things that she hated while she was working in a medical office because Teneil was not a people person. Lon didn't like women that were too smart so it was a giveaway when she went to work for this particular doctor. he and Mr. Deivers who she nicknamed "skin tight" had planned this all out. Mr. Deivers understood that out in those parts of the area where they looked for chocolate and then Lon could at least have phone sex with the doctor Teneil worked for because he seemed to like those dumb types. Teneil noticed this because his whole demeanor changed afterward. He was nicer and less hostile towards the family and was not in a bad mood where you walked on eggshells around him. She knew a white woman was all he needed to make him a happy idiot. Deep down she wished he would just go off and get with one so that he would be out of her life and no longer around to torture for everybody's salvation. Teneil knew he was a southerner who just didn't have the fortitude to marry who he wanted and to tolerate all that came with it. Lon had to use somebody as a buffer so that he would not be treated so mean by white folks and Teneil was just the one that he passed the buck to so that her father Lon could be that house negro and at least have this white friend that he always wanted.

"Hey, Lessy, it's good to hear from you. How are you doing?" asked Lon.

"Still behind bars, and still ain't seen my grandkids," said Lessy.

"I made sure you got them pictures of them and that corrections officer says you making him happy. said Lon.

"Yeah, thanks for hooking me up. I could use the clout in here cause this place is no joke. They gave me a life sentence for killing that boy. I got another several years to go before parole. But I am good for now. Just wishing to see my family more." said Lessy.

"Now, I know when your inmates get out of jail they are going to be our spies on the outside world so that we have people to use to lessen the blows, like taking it easy on you in jail or Lil Troy not having to do time at all. We can just put that off on people like Teneil. It's a public service thing that she needs to get through and life is like that in many respects we get called to duty in one form or another." said Lon.

"I want to thank you for what you did for Lil Troy while I'm in here. I'm really glad you could help me," said Lessy.

"Hey, anything for a buddy. We go way back and that was the least I could do. We types need to stick together so we can all make it through this. Who knows? The more we can get people to do the public service thing the more people we can get out of here and one day it can be you. Now, I'm working on this. I know you're a good person and deserve a high-paying job in some fortune 500 company making a lot of money. instead, you're behind bars because you're a black woman and if you were white you would have gotten off on an insanity charge. I mean this is crazy." said Lon as he felt a tightness in his chest.

"Yeah, and you are a good one for believing the way you do you know how some people depend on others." laughed Lessy.

"Yeah!" said Lon as he gasped for air.

"You, ok?" asked Lessy. "You seemed like you struggling to talk and I have never known you to be short on words or much else you always got something to say and never let anyone else get a word in," said Lessy.

"I am good. Just tired from all of the work I've been doing. I'm going to let you go now because I got to get back to what I was doing and you got to be careful to who hears your conversation up in there because we can't let them know what we got going on. We provide a service to people. Otherwise, we would never get what we want out of life and we have to be proud of what we are doing. Now you take care and I will speak to you soon." said Lon as he hung up the phone quickly.

He held his chest and took a few deep breaths and he thought about that woman Teneil worked for and wished he could have married someone like her. He would have left the big city and moved South and bought a mobile home and live off of half of what he makes now if he were able to do so. All Teneil wanted him to do was to stop playing phone sex and leave so she could have her life back because he made her miserable. Lon looked at his cell phone and thought to himself, 'Yup in my next life it's going to be all white." he felt a sharp pain and fell over.

"Girl, did you hear that noise?" asked Latrina as she was on the phone with Jacel.

"What noise?" asked Jacel.

"It sounded like something fell over. I know it wasn't a book because Lon just uses those for decorations." laughed Latrina.

"I didn't hear anything," said Jacel.

"I just did, and you best hope it ain't him sneaking out of the house to go roping around phone sexing on his company phone. You don't know what they got going around these days. Now go check I will stay on the phone with you." said Latrina.

Jacel walked up the steps and she saw Lon slumped over. "Lon, Lon!" she yelled.

"I told you girl I heard something." shouted Latrina.

"He is not answering me! yelled Jacel.

"Call an ambulance with the other phone, I will stay on the line with you." said Latrina.

Chapter Thirty

"Yes, thank you for telling me Jacel," said Mr. Deivers. "I know you will miss him dearly and I must say that I have never met anyone like him."

"Neither have I," said Jacel tearfully.

"Give my condolences to the girls and Lon Jr.," said Mr. Deivers. "I know they are grown and doing the work that their father wanted them to. Lon Jr. may not understand but he is in a group home and I'm sure they will help him along."

"It's been an eventful few days, I'm making the arrangements and I will send them to you once all is finalized," said Jacel.

"Yes, and I will tell Valdena Plantation also. I saw her a few days ago and she asked about the girls and of course Lon Jr.," said Mr. Deivers.

"Oh, and please tell her. Thank you, Mr. Deivers, for everything," said Jacel.

"No problem and call me if you should need anything," he said smugly as he hung up the phone.

Mr. Deivers looked around nervously. It seemed that as everyone got older, they had begun to break down. Mr. Deivers knew he has lost a valuable informant to their organization. Lon Sr. knew many people who aspired to be someone and managed to see to it that they became nothing but field helpers in the world of business. He was organized, he was slick and he knew how to talk to people, and knew how to convince people to believe what he told them. So people often did what he suggested and for many then ended up in places either South or jobs that were just the same. Lon Sr. knew how to be the tunnel that people would go through for advice. Many had either come from difficult homes or from parents who never gave their children much thought after a certain age. Lon Sr. knew how to take advantage of this to keep the fields of employment alive as though they were in the past. The invaluable information he told people about those who were struggling to succeed would become part of the information that the Klan used to thwart such efforts and use them for their own. It was so easy for people like Mr. Deivers to take others like Teneil and use them for such a purpose because society was not ready to handle integration in a world deemed perfect. Due to imperfections people like Mr. Deivers found other ways to use minorities. Mr. Deivers then picked up the phone and called Kib who had since retired from work and although still part of the Klan he had passed on the duties to the younger generation.

"I suppose you heard the news," said Mr. Deivers.

"Yeah, I heard. It is all over town. I can't imagine what stress he was under because he was the house negro. But then again he struggled to be who he was or felt trapped in his skin so to speak. It just slowly ate away at him." said Kib.

"You know this for sure?" asked Mr. Deivers.

"It ached at him not to be with his first wife Elkin or to spend time. He met some young thing around Teneil's age and has been chatting it up discreetly with her as you know Teneil works for her and that woman is just his type. He just being flirty with her and I think that was the only thing that kept him going. Lon Sr. never liked them too smart." said Kib

"So all of this worked in our favor. " said Mr. Deivers "I mean using people like Teneil."

"Yeah, but with Lon gone, we may lose track of others we can also use." said Kib."But we have the next generation of agenda."

"Who knows..." laughed Mr. Deivers, "Working apart as in from home might be the best solution..."

...

Teneil wiped her eyes as she felt as though she cried her last tear. Teneil was tortured, she felt abused and at times physically and emotionally exhausted. But with her father gone, there was hope for the future or what was left of it. She was older and a lot wiser in life and things had certainly taken their toll. It felt like some awful joke that her father was playing by taking a simple EEOC complaint and showing Teneil that civil rights didn't matter as if they were just words on a paper without meaning because the actions of others could not be prevented. So he taught her a lesson by making her work in a small office with a Klan member who of course hired somebody who was of no real assistance to the office. It was cruel to take something so meaningful from someone just to use it and make it into your desired agenda or the way you want life to exist. Teneil felt harassed, used, and enslaved without any rights available to help her and to be left alone by the people who despised her. Her father Lon was dead and after all, he was the one who blackballed her for the sake of him being the house negro and feeling young again by being able to chat it up with someone that reminded him of his first wife. Lon was educated on the outside but he was comfortable with mother as they say and living off the fat of someone else. That was the man Teneil knew. She knew a man who hated who he was and favored those who showed hate towards his people. An Uncle Tom or house negro. He was a man who concealed his anger at times and showed showed through his children. He resented having people who looked like him and that was why he did what he did resentfully and to of course have pawns to use in the establishment. Teneil was tired and finally free but she had wished her parents would not have used her as a martyr for the promiscuous and as a person of justice when one needed salvation and certainly not to prove a point such a purpose in life or duty, just one huge burden. Lon had managed to work a few years past his retirement age and earned a good salary. Lon and Teneil were opposites born on the opposite side of the tracks. She knew her father hated music because he always seemed to want to interrupt her or bother her when she wanted to play or listen to it. Teneil wanted her own home to be who she wanted to be and not have her parents dictate what career she wanted to appease somebody else ignorance. With her father now gone perhaps she could do that, although she had to help her mother around the house because Jacel could not get it together with a computer. She smiled because the fear she had of him was gone. She remembered asking him as she graduated high school was this a dilemma in life and he told her no. Strangely enough, Teneil knew not to believe him. The money to pay the bills was there and she said to herself, "Certainly not today and definitely not tomorrow. Right now, I just want to listen to some music."

www.ingramcontent.com/pod-product-compliance
Lightning Source LLC
Chambersburg PA
CBHW071249130626
46556CB00003B/1232